MIRRORS

K.S. WELLS

crippledbeaglepublishing.com

Cover design by Kat Vancil

Paperback ISBN 978-1-958533-00-0
Hardcover ISBN 978-1-970037-99-9

Follow K.S. Wells on Facebook

Disclaimer: While certain elements of this book were inspired by real life (isn't all art?), this story and its characters are works of fiction drawn from the author's imagination.

Mirrors

Mirrors. What to do with them. I looked in the mirror at my baby doll dress with the vertical blue stripes. Stripes must always be vertical. I saw that I was back to wearing high heels, even during the day. Every morning, I spent time to make sure my hair and makeup were done without looking *too* done. My new lifestyle leads to lunch with a friend in hopes that I meet a man while I'm there. I must be viewed and admired before he asks me out.

Divorce. Who would have guessed that at fifty years old, after spending half my life loyal and dedicated to one man, that I would be wearing vertical stripes, made up, styled, and walking out into a world of dating? Or should I say a world of *trying to date?*

Mid Life Course Correction. That sounds like the right terminology. I walked into the restaurant with confidence. I wanted men to look but was petrified they would. The overwhelming thoughts of, *Do I have what it takes to be attractive and sexy? Will someone want to touch me and love me? Screw me?* Such a dichotomy. After speaking for an hour, hearing about the kids' school and all that was wrong in my friend's world, lunch ended. I carefully got up from the table, made sure that my high heels didn't cause me to wobble and fall, and walked with slow, swinging hips past a table of six businessmen. *Are they looking? Yes, they are very much looking! Okay, confidence. Make eye contact and smile,* I silently thought.

The smile. I've been told I have a million-dollar smile. I reminded myself to accept my gifts and forget my flaws. I tried to swagger past the men, and what did I do? I avoided eye contact and kept moving. I felt their eyes watching me. Maybe so many eyes were watching that I panicked. Maybe I was just a chicken shit. I stood outside the restaurant but near the window in front of the table of businessmen. I fantasized that one of them would walk outside and introduce himself to me. Surely one of those men was single. I talked with my girlfriend for a while. No man came. Nope. Not one. I jumped in my car.

Confidence. I never lacked the trait until my divorce. I asked myself, *How* can *I be naked with a man? My body—it has changed in the last few years. How did I get here?* I went from athletic to curvy to slightly overweight. Now, I wear anything that has the power to hold me up because gravity is the enemy. Two children came through and out of my body. I should have won awards not extra pounds. Skinny women my age make me want to vomit, and I mean skinny not healthy. Women should have women's bodies that are soft, voluptuous, and strong.

I knew the process back to my athletic form would take some time. Rihanna sings, "Shine Bright Like a Diamond." My diamond had been roughened around the edges, but the light, the hope, was there.

It was not like I hadn't been asked out in the last year. During my separation, I was hit on three times. Ah, suburban America. Once in a grocery store (after 5:00 PM, of course). Once in Home Depot. Once in a restaurant. Only one had potential. The good news was that I wasn't looking or trying to get attention. I also wasn't wearing a wedding ring. More than anything, when those men approached me, I felt like the universe winked at me. It felt good. Now, my story was different. Now, I was the hunter. I'd started thinking like a man.

Sex. That is all I think about these days. I'm on a sexual exploration with oddly heightened awareness. After that lunch, I walked down the sidewalk toward my car and looked at every man, wondering whether or not I'd fuck him. *Is he fuckable? Would I fuck him?* If the answer was a maybe or yes, I immediately looked at his left hand for the ring.

I have zero interest in married men. If I spot a ring, he is never to be thought of again. If there is no ring, I ask myself if I have the courage to approach. These were and are the daily questions.

Dare To Share

Okay, I will. I am fascinated with sex toys. Vibrators galore. I enjoy reading about them, ordering them, using them, and eventually naming them. All of them. Oh, but I'm getting ahead of myself. My vibrator hobby tells only the beginning of the new me, new identity, new sexuality, new exploration. I love the new me.

Dating. When I was ready to date, I told all of my girlfriends. I explained by using lingo from decades ago, like, "Keep a lookout," "Let me know if you know anyone," "What about your husband's work associates?" and the gamut. At some point, against my wishes, I joined the online dating world. With the first sign-up, I became so overwhelmed that I deleted my account within a week. The first meet and greet went well, though. There was a strong emotional connection. He was British, nice, gentlemanly, well-mannered, and a good conversationalist. I thought I would go out with him again. Sadly, one of my gifts was getting people to open up. He opened up and let slip that he was married. I reacted calmly, but that was the end of that.

Soon, I had a second date. I thought I was going to like this man because we talked and texted for a few days before going out. I was really hoping the chemistry would be there, but in the first minute I realized, *Nope. Not there for me.* He was good looking, attentive, kind, very interested in me, and off to a great start. As he walked me to my car, he told me he was going to kiss me.

Now, I was open to kissing at that point, even though I was out of practice. I wasn't sure I could remember how to French kiss, make out, or even have "good" sex. Thus, I was quite curious and ready. Therefore, I had every intention of kissing any good looking, unmarried man, even if I knew the relationship was going nowhere. Excited to be kissed, I was soon let down. He went in for the kiss.

I thought I'd feel his lips at first, but his tongue dove down through my mouth. I freaked out and pushed him away. I literally told him, "Dude, you went all in! No warmup, no kiss on the lips, and then went into the French kissing. Just all in!" I did not like it. But he was still willing to accommodate. We talked more and he decided to tell me his sexual fantasy.

I have no idea why men ever think such a conversation is appropriate on a first date. Ultimately, looking back, I think he may have been a sex addict. Anyway, he told me his fantasy was for a woman to strap on a dildo and do him up the ass. This was after admitting he had done just about everything else, sexually. I didn't care what his desires were, and I didn't judge them, but why in the world would he tell a complete stranger this? *Save it for your willing partner*, I thought. That ended the conversation for me. I told him I was closing the chapter on our story, and, again, he went in for a kiss, totally catching me off guard. I told him no, pushed him away, and said goodbye. He texted me for weeks. I never responded.

I had several good dates with nice men who weren't all weird. I like to think I have strong intuition and good judgment, yet I still got it wrong many times. I want women to know this. It's okay to make mistakes, learn from them, laugh at them, and move forward.

Nine Months After Divorce

Another party. They require so much work these days. The process of taking another shower, doing my hair——blow drying, styling, flat ironing—applying makeup, stretching on Spanx to hold up my body and smooth out my rolls … exhausting. Then I have to muster the energy to make it past 10:00 PM. I've learned to drink caffeine around 5:00 PM so I can make it through the nights I go out.

I had to choose the right dress for this party. My options were the strapless, form-fitting, dusty rose number that fell right above the knee or the short-sleeved black one (out of twenty in my closet) that didn't cling but did show off my breasts and legs. I've always liked to leave something to the imagination.

Heels. I hate high heels. They are incredibly uncomfortable at my age. When you raise kids for twenty straight years, you get accustomed to Birkenstocks and tennis shoes so you can run at any moment. I had beige high wedges for the pink dress and black, high, strappy shoes for the black dress. That decision took another twenty minutes. I went with the dusty rose dress. I put on my makeup but not too much. I like to look natural, not fake, so I added only concealer, bronzer, eyeliner, eye shadow, mascara, and lipstick. That's it. Of course, I wore contacts and not glasses. I drove almost two hours to my dear friends' home on Lake Oconee for their yearly celebration. The driveway wraps around the home, which is hidden from the street. Their entry, with the larger-than-life arches, is beyond impressive. My friends never do anything halfway.

The house is amazing and enormous. My friends always create an exciting time. The diversity of the guest list that evening brought enjoyable conversation and laughter. We danced, ate delicious food, and drank from the open bar. Oh, how I love my girlfriends. How lucky I am to have them! They kept me sane as I went through my divorce. They lifted me up when I wanted to sink into bed. I thank God every day for them. I pray every woman alive find and keeps faithful friends. They are everything.

Events and parties are easy for me these days. I drive everywhere so that I can control when I arrive and when I leave. Freedom in my life is one of the most important gifts I have now. I won't let anyone or anything take that from me. One reason I can go to parties and drive home at any hour is that I gave up alcohol for a year. It was a big life change but one I will never regret. I gave up drinking two weeks before my separation because I realized that my stressful divorce could easily send me down a toxic rabbit hole. I didn't want alcohol to have a hold on me and decided it was more important to keep my wits about me than say something regrettable after having one too many. Dumping alcohol was one of the best decisions of my life. Little did I know how not drinking would benefit me in so many other ways.

I started with a challenge, motivated to take care of myself during the separation and divorce. I felt so much better that the weeks became a year. I joined a support group of women doing the same thing, and they became like sisters. We cheered each other through all the highs and lows of life. More than anything, along with my girlfriends, that support group got me through my divorce. I never realized that connection was the antidote to so many unfilled holes in my heart. I cherished those women. I became aware of how powerful women are in this world. That first year was a roller coaster ride. I could write a book about everything I went through in that time. What's important now is that if I could drop alcohol, even with all the pain and suffering I was enduring, then anyone can. So now, going on my first year post-divorce, parties are not a problem.

That evening, I walked in, found the bar, and ordered my own beverage that looked like an alcoholic drink. My preference is soda water with cranberry juice on the rocks in a small glass with two limes. The sugar gives me the energy to get through the night, and I stay in complete control and at peace knowing I can drive home whenever I want. That's powerful. That's freedom.

At the party, I immediately noticed that the majority of guests were couples. I threw air hugs and kisses to all I knew as I strolled around the outside patio. The pavers appeared endless. I looked up at the full moon shining over the lake. I mingled and began introducing myself to strangers.

I'm an introvert at heart; however, my family was filled with extroverts. They socialized and had parties all the time. There was zero tolerance for my being shy. I was expected to be outgoing, social, friendly, and offer a strong handshake with a smile. Those lessons and expectations, though uncomfortable, were a fantastic gift from my parents. I know no stranger, can chat with anyone, can easily initiate conversation, and am friendly, warm, and funny.

As an introvert, the day after a party means sleep and recouping the energy from my "fake it to make it" routine. I bet people think, *Look at her. She has a great personality.* Maybe I do, but I love quiet time. Remember the gifts your parents give you in life. Focus on the good things, and you can better heal from the bad things that didn't work in your favor during those formative years. Every child learns good and bad from his or her parents. I choose to perpetuate the positive.

Soon, I found my close friends in order to get the comfort and support I needed. They were all couples. They have all been married so long that all the girls huddle together while the men stand nearby but not in the inner circle. My girls look out for me. They make sure I don't sit alone and that I'm talking to someone. If I am alone, they show up by my side. They make sure I feel safe. They know I'm strong and independent, but no one is totally confident in life (even if they can fake it). Embrace this love. Be there for the divorcee. So many are not brave enough to venture out of their comfort zones. Invite them, make them go out, make the time. You never know how much it can change someone's life for the better.

After gaining momentum from my girlfriends, I ventured out to meet new people. Most people had enjoyed at least one or two drinks by then, so they were beginning to loosen up and become friendlier. When I wanted to join a conversation, I literally put myself in a circle if it's not too tight. I will sit down with strangers and open a conversation topic. It's not easy, but no one said life was easy. Most of the time it works; sometimes it doesn't. Either way, I know in fewer than five minutes whether to stay or leave that circle. I don't infiltrate a group of men, ever, unless they are my friends' husbands I know well. I will join couples or other women. I never want to look like a threat or competition, a.k.a., the end of friendships with women. I stay away from married men and never compete with another woman. Everyone loses. Period.

I spent about an hour talking, floating around, laughing, making connections wherever possible, and then the dancing began. As soon as the song started, I followed my girlfriends onto the dance floor. What woman doesn't love to dance with girlfriends? There is a childlike innocence and a ton of fun. I smiled the entire time. The outside patio was packed with people dancing all around. After some time, I needed a break and to cool down, so off I went to get water and take a brief walk around the property by myself.

The property has many concrete paths down to the lake. I took the long one through the trees. The air was so quiet I could hear only muffled music and laughter. I love nature. It calms me, grounds me, and gives me peace. I found myself in front of the lake. I took off my shoes to stand in the grass and breathed the fresh cool air deeply while I stared at the bright moon. I absorbed the moon's energy. I inhaled and exhaled, slowly calming my body so I could balance from the high energy of the party. I lost my thoughts and sense of time. When I turned to go back, I noticed a man standing behind me, but not too close. He was staring. *Interesting*, I thought. I usually can pick up on someone looking at me pretty quickly, but I didn't feel his eyes at all. I must have really been deep in my head.

My shoes were near him, so I slowly walked up, smiled, and said, "What a beautiful night and wonderful party." I giggled from a tad of embarrassment. As I came nearer to him, I could see his face. I always search the eyes first. They truly are the window to the soul. Eyes tell me if a person is kind, generous, open, loving, cold, controlling, or has a psychological problem. The only ones who throw me for a loop are the deep deceivers, the chameleons. They trick everyone and are some of the hardest to ever know. But this guy, was smiling wide with sweet, kind, blue eyes. *Wow*, I thought, *He's hot. He's about five-ten.* I prefer taller but that's good enough. He was slim, but not skinny, his clothes fit nicely, and he looked in style but not over the top. He had brown hair with tads of silver going through it and a medium dark skin tone. There are three physical traits that attract me the most in a man. His eyes, his smile—teeth cannot be messed up, and his height checked the boxes. That's about it for me. Everything else I can accept. I prefer a man who is in shape, but I don't mind his being somewhat overweight (as long as he isn't lazy). I really don't care about muscle heads because they are more into themselves than me. I love a giver.

I smiled warmly at him, giggled, and apologized that I didn't know he was there while I was lost in my mind. I rambled more about the party as I reached for my shoes. He just kept smiling and not saying anything for a moment, which made me giggle more. (I giggle when I'm uncomfortable or embarrassed, which makes me more embarrassed.) When I brushed past him, I felt his energy and was drawn to him. I pick up energy quickly from others. There was a draw for me from him. He finally spoke, calmly and gently saying, "I've been watching you tonight. You were quite interesting. I saw you come down here and was curious to know what you were doing, so I followed—not to be creepy. I wanted to introduce myself to you. I'm Jax."

"Oh," I said, "I'm not sure if I should feel flattered or creeped out, but I appreciate your honesty."

He laughed.

What a wonderful laugh. So sincere. He's lighthearted. That's a good trait to have. As I picked up my shoes, he told me to wait because something was in my hair. "Don't panic, but let me get it out for you."

I didn't move, paralyzed by the thought that some monstrous bug from the lake had landed on me. He moved close to me, very close. I could feel his energy. It was intoxicating. Electrifying. I took a deep breath, trying to absorb his presence. Something stirred within me. He told me to lean my head down toward him as he reached up to remove whatever was in my hair. At this point, time stood still. I was inches from his body—I smelled him. Our bodies could touch if we moved only a couple of inches. As he reached to remove the beast from my hair, something came over me. A total lack of impulse control. I placed my hand around his waist and pulled him closer to me. I laid my head sideways on his chest and held him. I had never in my life done anything like that to a stranger. It felt so natural. I let go of my thoughts, social conditioning, and limitations. At that moment, he wrapped his hands around me and held me close. Just like that, he reciprocated. He didn't say a word and offered nothing but acceptance to me, a stranger. He felt natural to me, like this was always meant to be.

That moment in time felt like we had been together for years, even though we had just met. I breathed it all in, stayed present in the moment, and then I freaked out. I pulled back. He let go. Immediately, I was in a state of shock at how inappropriate this scene was. I started talking. No, apologizing. Fast. I fumbled through my words. He just looked at me and smiled. Not a word. I talked more and made a bigger fool of myself. I stepped way back, moving six feet away so I was out of his energy field. I grabbed my shoes to run away. It was time for me to leave the party.

But as I came up from grabbing my shoes, he was right next to me and still smiling. He was killing me. I had no idea what to do, and I kept telling myself to shut up. Finally, I just stood there, paralyzed with embarrassment.

He moved directly in front of me, close, and said, "I'd like to get to know you better. I want to take you out."

Like an idiot, my mouth fell slightly open, and nothing came out. I was so shocked I couldn't say anything.

He smiled and said, "I'll need your number now."

He stepped forward to come within inches and said, "I'm going to kiss you now." He placed his hands around my face. I froze. He told me to close my eyes. I did. I could not believe my behavior. I didn't know this man. I felt his breath on my face. He was smelling me, taking his time. He kissed me on the forehead, then the nose. I held my breath, but my breathing, inhaling and exhaling, was so rapid that I couldn't control it. He moved down to my lips.

Ever so softly, ever so gently, ever so teasingly, he brushed his lips on mine with a feather kiss. He released his hands and stepped back as I opened my eyes to see him smiling again. Suddenly, I felt calm but excited. I didn't know what to do or how to react, but he did. He said, "Pick up your phone and text me." He gave me his number. I followed instructions. Whatever he told me to do, I did without thinking. "What is your name?" he asked.

"Skye," I informed him.

Now he had my number, my name, and my life in his hands. He said, "Skye, it appears you are about to leave. I'd like to walk you to your car."

I began to walk, taking the long way around, doing the Irish goodbye to avoid the crowd. He walked close beside me. I felt his energy emitting—intense, sexual, yet comfortable. Soon, he was reaching for my hand. He held it as we walked to my car.

Once there, what do I say? I thought. Such moments are so awkward. *Do I thank him, kiss him, make love to him, say, "Hope to hear from you?"* Weird. Luckily, I didn't need to say anything. He walked directly in front of me, said he was thrilled to meet me, and that he would see me soon. Then he firmly embraced me. He gave me a quick kiss, opened my door, helped me inside, and then watched me drive off.

I had an hour and a half drive home. I couldn't think of anything but him. The way he kissed me. His smile. His kind, twinkling eyes. Then the never-ending questions hit me. *Is he a player? He's good looking enough to be and smooth as butter. What's his story? Is he single or dating 1,000 other women? Why did he follow me? How long was he watching me from a distance? Will he call, or is this a fleeting moment for him?* Oh, how we women drive ourselves mad with these questions.

But then my mind went to other areas. *That kiss was so sensual. Is he like that in bed? Touching, feeling me all over, taking his time, being present in the moment? Will he romance me to death only to get me in bed and decide it's time to move on. Does he like the chase?* I could only imagine what it would be like to be with him. And all I knew was that I wanted him.

It was a fast drive home despite the distance. My mind was consumed in thought. At midnight, I walked into my house. My dog, Pepper, was so excited to see me that she did her usual greeting: whining and talking. I wondered what she would really say to me if she could put those sounds into human language. I loved on her and then took her outside. She's older now and doesn't like to be alone for long periods of time. I felt bad because I'm busier now and out more, so she's alone a lot more often. But as most dogs do, she loves and forgives me for living my life. I ripped the heels off first, then dropped the dress on the floor as I washed the makeup off, brushed my teeth, and readied for bed. I cuddled up to Pepper, rubbing her belly and telling her how much I loved her so she could be at peace to sleep.

She was settled, but I was not. I was about to turn my phone off for the night when I saw a new text. Jax. He asked if I made it home safely. Oh, I love that in a man. I love a man who wants to protect and keep a woman safe, caring about her. That went on his win list. He emphasized his excitement in meeting me, and I surmised that he followed up with the hosts to learn more about me. They have been dear friends of mine for twenty years, so I knew that great things were said. Farzeen would get a prompt call from me in the morning. I needed to know more about him. I don't like playing games with people in general, so to have the debate on whether or not I texted him back wasn't a question. Immediately, I wrote back to him, letting him know I was safe at home and thanking him for his sweet concern. I told him I looked forward to hearing from him again. That was the easy part.

But my mind was racing. I couldn't sleep. I was cozy and comfortable in my bed. My thoughts went to fantasies about Jax. I jumped out of bed and pulled my sex toys from their hiding place. I laid all five of them out in alphabetical order. Yes, I name my vibrators. And I love them. They are like having sex with different men many times a day. I thought, *I need to name one of these Jax.*

I have my favorite, but I wasn't sure I could change that name yet. My favorite is the first one I got while separated because it gave me such a thrill the first time I used it. *No. No changes to that one. Sentimental thoughts and high expectations are attached to that one.* I look at it like I'm a princess in a fairy tale and the vibrator is my prince. Perfect, he never lets me down and always satisfies and completes me. So, I really could never change that name because that is my fantasy, the perfect one, and Jax is a human. He's bound to let me down at some point. So, the name Jax was assigned to my second favorite one. It is above average size with ridges all the way around. It has a very small but effective knob for clit stimulation. It takes me longer to reach orgasm than some of the others, but the orgasms are large and long. Deep. With women my age, lubrication is key. I lubed up my Jax vibrator. Lying down and thinking about his kiss, the wet flow of excitement easily came. Slowly, in and out, I began as my mind went only to Jax.

I imagined him kissing my mouth, my neck, methodically touching my entire body from top to bottom, teasing me, tempting me with anticipation of what he would do next, until the thoughts of his penetration went deep inside me. And off I went. My orgasms have become unbelievable, stronger than ever before. I think I'm experiencing a sexual awakening beginning at fifty years old. Then, I was able to peacefully sleep after satisfying myself and thinking of fairy tales in my creative little mind. I said aloud, "Goodnight Jax," for I wanted him and would try to manifest him into my life.

Early

I'm an early bird. Waking up hours before dawn, I can do a ton of things with the clearest mind while sipping on hot coffee. I cherish my mornings in peace. I've created space in these mornings—for coffee, writing, prayers, meditation, yoga stretches, and opening my chakras while nude. This is one benefit of living alone. Nudity. It took a bit of time to get used to, but nudity is a condition I'm comfortable with now. We women have such body issues all of our lives. It shouldn't be this way. Unfortunately, it still is. When I got divorced, I was ashamed of my body. Somewhat overweight at the time because I ate my emotions during the last three years of marriage, I packed on the pounds and used them as protection against sex with the eventual ex.

I stopped exercising after years of physical activity and sports caught up and told my joints, "No, you are not thirty years old anymore." I quit. I was in complete protection and survival mode for years, but now I'm free. That freedom gives me time. I am determined to feel confident in my body again, knowing how it once looked and felt. So, I am often nude in my morning routine, nude during sleep, nude in front of the full-size mirror. I am getting more and more comfortable in my body, the feel of it, the look of it. I try to see it from a man's perspective instead of mine. I realize that when I feel my body without looking, just feeling, I love the way it feels. My skin is smooth, my body is soft in all the places a man wants it to be. Comfortable.

When I look at it from a man's perspective, I'm gentler with the criticism. Yes, I could lose weight here or firm up there, but am I fuckable? The answer is always a yes. This builds a confidence that I lacked for too long. Truly, I wish all women of all sizes would embrace their bodies with the utmost respect and confidence. If we are able to thank God for our bodies, how much healing could we give ourselves.

We could break free of the societal viewpoint that has never benefited us in any way. Oh, I plan on aging gracefully, but I have zero desire to try to look like I'm thirty when I'm fifty. I embrace my age with pride. I earned the scars, and I like a man who admires my imperfection.

After my very early morning routine, I always check my phone. I have learned to turn it off at night and resist looking at it the moment I wake. These small habits are healthy. However, my heart jumped a beat when I saw another text from Jax that early morning. He sent it late the night before. I wondered if he couldn't sleep or if he'd ended up jacking himself off to me while thinking of me at the same time I was taking care of my own business. A smile came to my face. Jax wrote that he'd love to see me today and was willing to come up to my area so we could spend the day together.

I thought, *Wow, a whole day … that seems like a lot*. But I decided to go for it. I would want to get to know him better. I mean, in these times, you have to eliminate that the guy is married, separated, a player, chaser, liar, sociopathic, psychopathic, has mental disorders, stalkers, control freaks … I could go on and on. Many questions needed to be eased into conversations without me looking like a lawyer or private investigator. That would take time. I thought it was way too early in the morning for a response on my part. Thinking about what we would do for an entire day at the last moment was too much. *Maybe I'll suggest lunch instead.*

At a more appropriate time on that Sunday morning, 8:00 AM, I texted him back saying how great it was to meet him last night. I told him I was intrigued by the connection, and I'd love to get together with him sometime that day. "What do you have in mind?" I texted.

19

The dots showed up immediately, and he responded almost instantly. I loved it. What woman doesn't like a man who's interested and seems like he is waiting to hear from her? It's important to show attention to a woman. He wrote back, "Good morning beautiful. You've already made my day by getting back to me. I've thought about you all night. I had trouble sleeping and hoped to hear from you this morning."

Interest. Attention. Sweet words. I was impressed. I texted, "Ahhh, that is so sweet." I waited to see what he would propose we do that day. I hoped he wasn't the type of man who likes the woman to make all the plans. Been there, done that. Yes, ask me what my thoughts are, and yes, sometimes I'll make the plans, but please send me a real man. I want a man who will chase me, one who will initiate. I thought, *Please, oh please, be a man, Jax.*

The Man Plans

He was a man. At least, at the first check. He asked me if I'd been to the Georgia Aquarium. I responded that I hadn't been in years but love animals. He responded back asking if I'd liked to join him that afternoon and then go to dinner afterwards. I hesitated in my mind. *This will be all day. This is walking together, talking a lot while in the aquarium, then dinner could be two more hours of conversation.* For me, that felt like a lot for a first date.

Then I thought about the night before. The instant connection I felt for this man that I'd never met. There was chemistry on my part and I certainly was curious. I was not one-hundred percent sure what I wanted to do, so I thought about it for five minutes or so, and before I responded, he texted back almost like he'd read my mind. "You're probably thinking this is a lot of time with someone you just met. Please allow me to say it is my intention to get to know you much better, and time is valuable. I want to spend this time with you."

Well, that did it for me. How could I resist? If it were an epic fail at the aquarium, I'd bail on dinner. There is always a way out. If the aquarium was great, then I'd want more time and conversation with him. So I said, "Yes, that sounds great. What time should I meet you there?"

He said, "I'll pick you up at 1:00 PM." Another holdup. I drive myself to dates. It gives me a sense of control and allows me to stay safe. I didn't know him, so picking me up at my house and knowing where I lived was a whole new ballgame. I texted back with the explanation that there was no reason for him to drive out of his way—he's in Brookhaven, I'm north of that—then backtrack to downtown.

Again, he read my mind. "If you prefer that I don't come to your home, then I can pick you up in a public shopping area. I just want to pick you up because I'm old-fashioned that way."

If I allowed this, I couldn't bail on dinner. Thinking, projecting what could happen, I sensed being out of my control and comfort. *Do I trust him? Dig deep, Skye. What is your intuition telling you?* I needed to meditate more. So, I messaged, "Meeting at 1:00 sounds great. Allow me a bit of time to get back to you on how we meet."

After that, I got off the phone. I sat down and began my meditation. The forms I had tried for decades and failed at are now my lifesavers. "When the student is ready …," I guess. As I went into my meditative state and let go of all the noise in my head, I relaxed and allowed the universal energy to flow through me, calm my body, ease my mind, and cool my emotions. I realized that this situation was exactly what the universe had sent, quite literally, walking into my life. Who am I to push back? Once I came out of my state of being quite calm, I let him know what shopping center I'd meet him at and that I looked forward to spending the day getting to know him better. I left it in the hands of the universe.

Jax replied, "That works great." Then he finished by saying he was excited to know me better as well. What I liked about him during those texts was that he allowed me the time I asked for and waited until I responded. He showed emotional intelligence. That is one of the most important traits I look for in a person. When I replied, he responded immediately, but he waited for me. He gave me the respect and time to think and react. This was good stuff. And so it began.

Jaxson, a.k.a., Jax

Like most people in modern times, I began to snoop a little about this new person. Social media checks began. From what I read, Jax was fifty-one years old and grew up in the Atlanta area with Persian parents. He was in the healthcare business (nothing specific was mentioned), often traveled internationally for work and fun, was well dressed, was educated at Florida State University, and had zero pictures of a former wife or kids. I wondered if he'd ever been married or was just very private on the home front. From what I could see, he was about five feet and eleven inches tall with dark brown wavy hair with a nice blend of gray running through it. He had blue eyes and medium skin tone. He looked like he always had a tan. Lucky man. He had an average build with toned muscles.

When he smiled, his whole face lit up, and the small wrinkles around his eyes danced. His lips were full. I wanted to suck them. He didn't look like he went to the gym all the time, nor a spa, both of which I appreciate as a woman. Who doesn't want a man who takes care of himself? But no normal woman wants a guy who spends copious lengths of time trying to look twenty years old. We were mature adults. I expected gray or white hair (or no hair), wrinkles and crinkles, not-so-tight muscles, and a belly. I also appreciate men, like women, who cover their physical flaws and flaunt their assets without being obsessive. Classy. Yes, I like class, but I also want a wild side dedicated just to me. It is a difficult, delicate balance to find a unicorn in a world full of toads.

I thought it was time to call my girlfriend, Farzeen, the one who had the party, to find out the real scoop. Of course she picked up; she had obviously been waiting for my call and wanted the details. She began, "So, my love, you disappeared during the party, and we didn't say goodbye. The next thing I know, Jaxson appears next to

23

me, thanking me and stating he's leaving but would love a moment to discuss someone he met. Of course, at first, I had no idea about whom he was talking. Intrigued, I gave him all of my attention and time. When he started to describe this gorgeous woman with long brown hair, a smile that commands attention, and eyes that dance, I knew she was you. Then he went on and on about you, and I knew he was hooked. So we walked a tad away from the party and sat down. He wanted to know everything about you. I told him how we've been close friends for about twenty years, how we met through our kids, and how we share family values and life. How you were kindhearted, strong, and independent. How sad we were to learn of the divorce but understood that your paths were going separate directions and that you're friendly with your ex. That you are a catch. That only a very special man will be welcomed into your world. One who is attentive, kind, generous, and fun. On and on I went, explaining how perfectly wonderful you are."

After I thanked her, I immediately asked her what the story was with Jax. I told her to be direct. I learned that Jax was born in America. He came from wealth and would continue a successful family legacy. Money was no problem. I found this to be true of most of my Persian friends in America. They are both inherently wealthy and tend to be even more successful on their own accord in this country. Some of the wealth astounds me. Money is wonderful. It buys freedom. Other than that fact, it is not something that is hugely important to me. She described his family as loving, supportive, and also demanding of Jax. She said he has one sibling, a sister who is married with children. I asked if he'd been married or if he had children. She told me that he had been married but got divorced with no children. Farzeen explained that all she knew of the marriage was that it lasted for ten years, and he was devastated when it ended. He went hog wild (like most recently divorced men I know) for the first couple of years following the divorce, partying and fucking everything in sight. She said that he'd been divorced for about five years and that he'd settled his wild oats, it seemed, for the most part. He'd had a serious relationship that lasted a year, but he ended that, and the woman was crushed.

My thoughts went into overdrive. *Great, he's a heartbreaker. Not what I need. BUT … Farzeen says he is hardworking, kind, generous, attentive, a great conversationalist, educated, well-liked in their community, and all the women want him.* Being friends for as long as we had been, I asked her if I should go out with him. Her answer was, "Yes, oh yes, you are a great match. But Skye, my dear, be careful with your heart. You need to find out his intentions with you. I don't want him to break your heart. That is the last thing you deserve." It was a fair warning and one that I would remember. In the meantime, I was more than intrigued to get to know this mysterious Jax.

Ready

What the hell was I going to wear? We were going to the aquarium, so I needed to be casual with tennis shoes, but for dinner I needed a sexy dress with heels. Shit. I was running out of time and hadn't thought this through. So I texted Jax, "Any idea where we might have dinner? I have no idea what to wear, since I'll need comfortable shoes for the aquarium and possibly an outfit change for dinner." I believe in being honest and authentic. If he took my approach as high maintenance, so be it. He didn't. He said to wear comfortable clothes for the aquarium and to bring a cute outfit, not dressy, to change into for dinner. Shit, not what I wanted to hear. That was more complicated for me. I'd need makeup adjustments, hair adjustments, etc. Men don't think about such things from a woman's perspective. For example, where the hell would I be changing? So I texted, "Will do, but where am I changing?"

His response was "Keep it simple. I've got you covered. It's not a problem." Vague. I didn't like that but have worked hard on releasing my constant need for control. I thought, *Fine, I'll take a dress bag with shoes and a small bag with touch-ups.* And what defines the difference between a cute outfit and a dressy outfit? Perception? This was like mind reading. I took his answers at face value and up one notch so as not to be underdressed. I hoped for the best. What I did know is that Persian men appreciate beauty. I needed to play up my looks.

I looked at the time. Where did it go? I took Pepper for a quick walk and grabbed something substantial to eat so I wouldn't get hangry. Grouchiness is a negative trait to display on a first date and in general. Men need to feed their women and not let them get hangry.

Then the prep work began. I felt tension. Nervousness. I needed to get that energy out. I'm big on energy release. Other than exercise, I prefer sexual release. I threw off my clothes. I grabbed my bag of tricks, a.k.a., vibrators. Which one would I choose? I thought, *I'll go with my first one, my favorite.* When I release sexual tension, I diminish my impulsive desires. I was not going to sleep with someone on the first date, so releasing before the date was insurance. I wonder if men jack off before a date to release that tension. Or do they jack off so they last longer if they *do* get lucky? Probably both. I need to ask a couple of my guy friends.

I had to be quick because I needed the time to get ready. My favorite vibrator gives me the deepest satisfaction along with fast orgasms. I lubed him up, lay down, and went into the world of fantasy in my mind. As I imagined some of my regular fantasies and tried to pin the one down that would help me climax quickly, I kept thinking of Jax. I was trying not to think of Jax. I didn't have anything to go on yet. But I couldn't help it. He had a strong sexual pull—one I hadn't felt for a very long time. I wanted to control this fantasy, but realizing that I couldn't, I decided to see where it went in my mind.

I thought about his smell when I first wrapped my arms around him. The dark, musky, almost woodsy combination of a mysterious scent that immediately sent a rush of wetness. Then his touch and my instinct to wrap my arms around a stranger. The move was so unlike me, yet some mysterious magnet pulled me to him. I couldn't resist. The desire arose. I thought about the slow, gentle teasing of his kiss. That kiss blew my mind. My body was so ready. My tits grew hard with anticipation. I was wet, so I turned the vibration on and slowly went to work. My mind moved forward from that kiss to him grabbing me, pulling me closer, his hands moving slowly but surely from the top of my head all around me. Pulling closer so not even an inch stood between us. I could feel him. I wanted him. He

27

started to kiss me softly at first, but his desire was there, too. That kiss went from soft to deeply passionate. Biting my lip as he came up for air, he moved down to my neck. Oh, the sweet spots all over the neck. I could have neck sex alone. Sucking, licking, kissing all around my throat, hairline, ears … then he turned me around to kiss the back of my neck. The best part is the back. He grabbed me closer, taking control. I submitted. Soon, I came with a huge release. I didn't even make it past the neck kissing in my fantasy. I could not imagine what future fantasies would look like—when he would go lower on my body. I thought I probably wouldn't make it five minutes before exploding.

I got lost in my fantasy world. Time flew by. I had to get ready. What to wear? *Okay, Jax, you've seen me dressed up. Let's see what you think about me dressed down.* I grabbed leggings, a nice T-shirt, and souped-up tennis shoes. I did my face and hair nicely so I could easily transition into evening. Then I thought about the change. Still not knowing where we were eating but guessing it would be nicer than casual, I went for the upscale casual look. I chose a cute, blue, mid-length, summer dress with high wedge, neutral-colored heels. I grabbed an oversized cardigan in case it got cold in the restaurant. The sweater was also a security blanket for me in case I felt vulnerable or exposed. I grabbed a dress bag to store the items and finished getting ready. I filled a small bag with makeup, a hairbrush, toothpaste, and a toothbrush to freshen up later. I tossed in a small perfume bottle as well.

I gave my pup a treat and a kiss because she would be hungry when I got home later. Off I went. I drove to the public parking place near my home to meet Jax. I pulled up, freshened my lipstick, and the next thing I knew, Jax was next to my car. Obviously, he saw me and was waiting. Good. I didn't want to wait for a man. I got out of the car. He had the biggest smile, which made my heart skip a beat. Desire permeated my being. I smiled back as he reached forward and pushed my hair away from my face. Wow, just like that, he touched without asking, without permission, like he was a part of me already. I let him. I liked seeing how and if I could submit to a man and what that felt like.

Jax was dressed in nice jeans, tennis shoes, and a slim-fit polo shirt. We wore similar clothing, so I didn't feel underdressed. He grabbed my things from the back of the car and loaded them into his blacked-out Maserati. That car made me wonder if he had a big ego. It was beautiful. He obviously did well or pretended he was doing well. Regardless, I wasn't impressed by his vehicle. He opened the car door for me and gently held my hand, lowering me into the passenger's side. I felt nervous and excited. I'm not sure which feeling was dominant. As he got into his side, he leaned into me. I was taken off guard. Was he going to kiss me? Take me? What was going on?

He looked me in the eyes and said, "I've been thinking about you non-stop, and I am so happy we are spending this time today together. You look beautiful. And I hope you will relax as the day continues."

Wonderful, he can tell I'm chicken shit. I took a deep breath because I needed to calm my nerves. I said, "Thank you. I hope I can feel more comfortable as well."

As we took off, he talked the entire time. I loved listening to him. His voice soothed me. He told me about his life—what he did, his hobbies, his travels. Then he told me how he felt when I touched him for the first time. He said he knew something was real between us. I was speechless, which was an oddity in itself, but I listened attentively and smiled warmly. The more he talked, the more I was drawn to him. Intriguing.

29

First Date

As we entered the aquarium, Jax gently took my hand in his. We took our time talking, laughing, and watching the exhibits. Throughout the day, I was amazed at how easily our conversation flowed. He kept moving closer to me as the day went on. At one exhibit, as I stood against a rail to watch the animals, he came up right behind me and placed his body softly against mine. He gently put his arm around my waist. So natural. He was certainly smooth. He stood close and leaned into my ear, whispering things about the exhibit. I could not even register what he was saying because his physical presence in my aura had me frozen. It was unbelievably sexy and sensual. Sensuality is the biggest turn on for me.

I wouldn't turn around to look at him for fear my desire would overcome my control. Eventually, I let him take me by the hand again as we continued. The date was the sweet kind during which you can learn about each other, sense if the relationship may go somewhere, and test if the physical chemistry is there. For me, Jax checked all the above boxes. I didn't know if he felt the same about me or if it was just a sex thing for him. He was super sexual. I knew this with every ounce of my being. It permeated him, flowing freely out into the universe. And he was confident.

We left the aquarium, and I wondered where I was going to be changing and freshening up. As if reading my mind, Jax said we were going back to his place, because it was near town, to get ready for dinner. Once again, my anxious mind freaked out. I was in his car not mine, so I had no exit strategy, and now we were going back to his place. In the past year, I'd gone to a guy's place only once. This was too vulnerable for me, too exposed, too open to things not going the way I wanted. I could not do or say anything other than place a small prayer that our going there was not his ploy for us to land in his bedroom.

We arrived at his townhome in Brookhaven. It was modern, with simplistic design and furniture, yet still cozy. I spotted few personal touches in typical bachelor style, but the place was very clean. It looked as though he almost didn't live there. As I complimented his home, he carried my things and walked me to the guest bedroom. He was a perfect gentleman.

He opened my car door, helped me out of the car and into his house, carried my things, and talked to make me feel comfortable. The date was so easy for him. Obviously, Jax had done this a thousand times with other women. He laid my things on the bed, turned to me, and said "Will an hour be enough time before we leave?" I said yes, that's plenty of time, and he quickly gave me a sweet kiss on my cheek yet right next to my lips. He left the room, shutting the door behind him. He had caught me off guard once again.

I sat down. Mentally, I was exhausted. I am such an emotional woman. I feel everything. I've learned to embrace this in myself and no longer allow anyone to squash it after so many years of men telling me to calm down, tone it down, stop being dramatic, etc. I ran from those men. They wanted to control or change me. I could not be free with them. And there are many men like that in this world. Jax wasn't one of them. It was almost like he knew these vulnerabilities and character traits in me and fed off them (in a good way), like he *wanted* me to release the emotions so he could absorb all of them. He was different. I sat on the bed, losing myself in my mind again, but I needed to put those thoughts all aside, relax, and get ready. I took some deep, calming breaths and prepped for the evening.

Once I was ready, I walked out to his main living area. I didn't see him, so what did I do? You could say I observed, but to be more accurate, I snooped. I walked around, looking at everything in the room and searching for books. I wanted to know his mind. There were few personal items, but I finally did find a room with books. I looked at them. Books tell you so much about a person. Most of his were classics that his interior designer, no doubt, put there for decoration. But, on the side of one shelf, there were a few well-worn books.

I was about to grab one when I noticed Jax standing at the door watching me. Again, I blushed. His intense stare caught me off guard. I wondered what he was thinking. Oh, how I would have paid to know his thoughts at that moment. He smiled and quietly asked if I was ready to go. "Yes," I said as I walked toward him. He didn't move from the door frame at first. He slowly reached up my arm and gently brushed on it. He told me I looked beautiful. I warmly thanked him and told him he cleaned up well. Sexy.

We laughed at dinner and whispered stories about our lives into each other's ears. The conversation was easy and fun. His eyes danced when he smiled. There was kindness but also mischievousness in his gaze. As the evening went on, I could almost finish his sentences. It seemed like our minds were melding into one. I felt comfortable. I felt like myself. I flirted endlessly with him, something I like to do, keeping in mind there was a thin line between innocently flirting and seriously seducing. After a wonderful two-hour dinner (the man didn't pick cheap), we headed back to my car. The day had been long, and I knew I would sleep well that night.

My mind went to letting the dog out and thinking of what was on my schedule tomorrow. Oh, the wonders of our minds. We try so hard to live in the moment but always look ahead. My demeanor had changed. Jax noticed. So, he started talking. He let me know he'd had a wonderful time with me, that he thought I was beautiful, and that he enjoyed our conversation. What I liked about Jax was that he sensed my shifts and accommodated me, meeting me exactly where I was. Clearly, he wanted me to understand he was interested. And that is very important to a girl. But he had to chase. I would not chase under any circumstance. I responded appropriately, giving him gratitude and reciprocation without going overboard. As he pulled next to my car, he turned the engine off. He looked at me squarely in the eyes. The intensity was there again. It excited me and made me nervous at once. I held his eyes to express that I was very interested. He asked if he could see me again that same week. I said I was sure that could be arranged, and I looked forward to it.

As I turned to open the car door, he grabbed my hand, so I turned back to him. Swiftly, like a lion after prey, he leaned over and kissed me. Just a kiss. Serious but sweet. He got out of the car, jogged around to open my car door, helped me out—what a gentleman—and opened my own car door for me. Before I climbed in, his body was right next to mine. Again, he was quiet and swift. So, when I turned, I was inches away from him, staring right into those eyes with so much character and depth. I felt flushed. I felt electricity between us. Sexual tension. I love sexual tension. He smiled, then took a step closer, wrapped his arms around my waist, and gently pulled me into his body.

He said, "I'm going to kiss you. Close your eyes."

I did. I waited. Nothing for a minute. I got nervous. Should *I open my eyes? No, just wait.* As soon as I was about to open them, I felt his hot breath on my neck … just slowly brushing up on my neck … not kissing.

Was he smelling me? It was like he was taking in my energy. Breathing me in. My body tensed. I was electrified. Up by my ear, his breathing, my tensing. Around my forehead, breathing, down to my cheek, breathing, and then I felt his breath near my mouth. He hovered. Then, softly, slowly, he kissed my lips. Just a kiss, no tongue, no jumping on me or down my throat, just a long, slow kiss.

33

Then release. Without thinking on my part, when he finished and before my eyes opened, I let out a soft moan. *Where the hell did that come from?* I embarrassed myself. I opened my eyes as he smiled down at me, and he said, "Talk soon, beautiful. Today was amazing." Speechless and stunned, I turned to get into my car. He closed the door.

I could not get out of there fast enough. I raced home thinking only about that kiss. Oh my gosh, this was what fantasies were about. If he kissed me like that, I could only imagine what other things he would do to me, taking his time, driving me crazy in the process. This was the first man I'd met since my divorce that I'd truly desired with my entire being—mind, emotions, and body. And just liked that, on a five-minute drive home, I decided without any doubt that I wanted him. All of him.

Available

I'd like to say that once I got home, I went straight to bed and slept. But after attending to my pup and getting ready for bed, all I could do was run the day through my mind. I picked up the subtle hints that I missed when they were happening. A review of the day gave clarity and perspective. But as I climbed into bed, I checked my messages. Nothing. I then turned my phone off, thinking he was probably not home yet, but I eventually tossed and turned trying to sleep. I couldn't. The energy was still there. I thought about that kiss.

Instantly, I got wet. This man understood that just a kiss could drive a woman wet with desire. He understood women. My only two criteria for a lover from the beginning and why I hadn't had one yet was emotional connection and fun. I'd met many men throughout that year who were fun, but they had no emotional connection with me.

Jax had both. I wanted him as my first lover after a long drought. That said, the thought of being naked in front of any man after being with the same one for twenty-five years, the thoughts of what to do sexually, not to mention if I even remembered what to do, and wondering if I even knew how to French kiss, were absolutely debilitating. How would my body respond? Would I be self-conscious about the areas that needed improvement? I'm older, with some extra pounds, cellulite on my ass and thighs, sagging skin here and there, and other issues my girlfriends and I talk about. What's the solution? Would I say anything about how or where to touch me?

We women have so many insecurities and doubts. I'm a confident person, but this area was out of my comfort zone. The first time would no doubt be less than great for me. I certainly wasn't going to climax because I doubted I could relax enough to have an orgasm. But at some point, one had to make the leap and dive in headfirst. That night, I did need to relax so I could sleep. So, my toys came out to play. Nothing beats releasing sexual tension and energy before sleep. I looked them over and decided my second favorite would be used that night. I renamed him Jax. This "Jax" vibrator was one that took me a tad longer to climax but gave me a deeper orgasm. I use it when I have more time to enjoy the experience. The vibration is average, not super strong, and its length is average with a slight curve. It has ridges on it and a small nub at the base for clit stimulation. This was how I wanted lovemaking to go with Jax if it happened—slow, consistent, deep. I lubed it up and began the replay with added fantasy of my day with Jax until I climaxed and fell fast asleep.

I woke up to a sweet text message from Jax, stating what a wonderful time he'd had with me and that he loved my smell and wanted to kiss me more. Then he asked when he could see me again. I'm a true believer if a man is interested, he chases and pursues. Jax was interested. So was I.

What to do? This is where I often get awkward. Does one play a game by not being easily available, or does one make sure she is available? Men say they don't like games, but I swear they play them more than any woman does. If a woman comes off as available, she's somehow less desirable, but if she plays too hard to get, the man loses interest. There's a fine line.

I'd worked so hard on internal strength and authenticity for the past two years. I went with *available*. However, I carefully and clearly responded, "I would love to see you again. What do you have in mind?" This way, I gave him the control and let him decide when to see me again. Available, open, and receptive.

He said, "Today." I smiled to myself because then I knew he was very interested.

Again, I carefully said, "I could do something this afternoon if that works." So date number two began that afternoon.

Second Date

That time, he came to my house with beautiful flowers in hand. As he arrived and I welcomed him in, he immediately came close to my face, grinning from ear to ear, staring into my eyes with intensity. He said nothing. He placed both of his hands around my face, pushed my hair back, and slowly pulled me into him as he reached down to kiss me. That kiss was different. At first, he kissed more intensely. Then he briefly looked at me, said, "Hi gorgeous," and went in for a real kiss. I felt completely helpless while my body grew intensely wet and my breasts got firm; the desire within me was coming up from a deep well.

Holding my face, he went into my mouth with his tongue, first a slow pace and almost liked he was checking it out inside. Then the craving took over as I responded completely. The next thing I knew we were in a full make out session, standing by the front door. His kiss made me want to scream with desire. He moved to the neck, a weak spot for me, as he continued to make my body come alive. I'd forgotten what it was to kiss so passionately. How a kiss can make one explode. Everything starts with the kiss. Pulling me closer and closer to his body, he began to move me in slow motion. We were a dance of two souls that had known each other for a lifetime. So natural, so easy, so much desire. I started to lose my thoughts as I embraced the physical sensations that I felt all over. Romantic.

All I knew was that I didn't want to move too fast. I enjoyed the chase, the romance, the sexual tension that came with dating. And I wanted him to want more; to think about it, to imagine, to have feelings for me, to build an emotional connection so he wouldn't leave me high and dry.

I become attached the moment I have sex with a man. I cannot separate my feelings from sex. I won't have it if my feelings aren't

38

there, so it was so important for me to have that person feel the same way about me. It doesn't need to be love or some form of unhealthy neediness. However, caring about the person and how they feel is key. At that point post-divorce, I wanted a sexual partner who was committed to me, alone, while we explored the potential of something more. I wouldn't have a partner who was sleeping with anyone else; I know my value, and I deserve more. Even in the raw aftermath of my divorce, I knew my worth. If it didn't work out in the long run, at least I wouldn't feel cheap or used. I could be an adult about it. I wanted a man, not a boy, with high emotional IQ who was fun and sensual. That was it. But I understood that it was still a lot to ask for in a man. If he could be vulnerable, then the connection could happen, for I'm all about emotions and feelings. Jax and I were not there, so I wouldn't give him or myself all that we wanted that afternoon.

I pulled back first. Looking into his eyes, I said, "That's the best greeting I've had in a very long time." I turned around to get my things so we could leave. He pulled me from behind and brought me next to his body. He was persistent. I'll give him that. I could feel how rock hard he was. This was going to be equally tough for me to resist. I didn't pull away. He pushed my hair to one side and kissed the nape of my neck. That is my Achilles heel. It was like he could read my mind and knew exactly where my weaknesses were. It was uncanny. I let out a moan and thought, *Where did that come from?*

He released me. I stumbled a tad, feeling off balance, as I made my way to place the flowers in a vase and get my things to leave. I didn't turn around to look at him because I felt so exposed, but I could feel him intently watching my every move, like a tiger about to mount his prey.

I walked toward him. He grabbed my hand to hold, and off we went. He opened doors for me, he brought flowers, he made me feel wanted. He gave me undivided attention. As a matter of fact, his phone was silenced when he was with me. He was one hundred percent in when we were together. I wondered if this would last or if he was a conqueror. He listened attentively and responded with relational understanding. He talked and shared about himself but not in a vulnerable way. I determined to see if I could change that. He drove us about an hour away to go hiking.

That day, he saw me as myself. In athletic wear. Tight workout pants, tennis shoes, and a fitted but not revealing shirt. I had grabbed a light sweatshirt to bring (another security blanket), a water bottle, a hat, and a ponytail holder in case I pulled my hair up. I wore very light makeup and sunglasses. This was how I really dressed and looked day to day, so it was better for him to decide now if he liked what he saw. However, after the initial entry, I learned he was perfectly fine with my down to earth style.

Jax assured me the hike wasn't too difficult. I was not into that. I love hikes to be strolls through nature, with fresh air to breath and surroundings to appreciate. I am not into a competitive feat of who can get to the top first. I had that in my first marriage. Everything was competitive. I was always being left behind. My husband was way ahead and yelling for the rest of us, kids included, to hurry up and pick up the pace. What was the damn hurry?

There was no easy affection, no talking, no partnership. I wanted to slow down, look at flowers, see the light coming through the trees, smell the air, look for wildlife, notice the smaller jewels of life and nature. I like to take my time, make stops along the way, sit by a river, or embrace a waterfall. I want to talk, hold hands, be a partner, and build a family. It is a blessing, God's world. I want to enjoy the present. Instead, my ex had us racing, pushing the kids to move it along. Over time, I became downright sad and angry all the time. Oh, how I begged God that Jax wasn't like my ex-husband. I could never go back to that life or lifestyle. It just about killed me.

As we arrived, again, it was like Jax knew what I was thinking. He sensed my hesitation. Whenever he picked this up in me, he started talking a lot. I liked it because listening to him talk calmed me down. His words distracted the tiring thoughts in my head. He really was good at that, and I was curious to find out how he became that way. He wanted to calm me, to make me feel safe and protected. There was something special in his being. I could easily fall in love with him.

We got out, he grabbed his gear, he quickly gave me a kiss, and he held my hand. We were in public, so big public displays were out for me, but affection is always welcome. After a quick bathroom break and staring at the map with Jax to decide which route was best for our first hike together, I let him decide. I just said I didn't want anything difficult or more than three hours round trip. He agreed and picked one. Holding my hand, he started the journey up the mountain through the forest. After about twenty minutes, the crowd dissipated, so he began to talk. He asked me how I was doing, which was fine, then began with questions. After the first couple, I stopped and said to him. "I love that you're trying to get to know me. I appreciate that, but let's make a deal. Every question you ask me, you have to answer as well. That way, I'm learning about you and on equal ground."

He laughed sweetly and said, "I love how you think. That will make me come up with better questions to ask." He started safe, asking me how I met Farzeen. Then he shared his side, how they met, how long ago, how they were friends, and I learned her husband was the connection. As we progressed the mountain, we progressed in questions. He asked about my childhood, my family, where I went to school, how I was in high school, then college, how I got to Atlanta, my first job, my career, my dreams. He shared all of that with me as well. We were learning about each other. Where the core values came into play, where things went right, where they

41

went wrong, what we learned, what were our experiences, what were our perceptions, and how those beliefs had changed or not. This was the good stuff. This was connection.

We paused along the way many times to take in the smells of the forest, dropping the heavy stuff for a moment to enjoy the journey. For me, this was what it was all about. Sharing, connecting, partnering. We laughed many times, and we stopped often to reflect in silence. He held me close from time to time, not saying anything but embracing the present moment. He gave me brief kisses of affection, not sexual in nature. This made me relax with him. It felt like we'd been together for a while.

I needed to keep myself in check, though. This was brand new. My guard could come completely down so soon. But he, like me, was building upon something. We were both curious about each other, which was healthy and good. I soaked him completely in, and I could not remember feeling that way about anyone in a long time. I enjoyed his company. I liked his personality and most importantly, I liked myself when I was with him.

As we neared the top of the mountain, he asked me how I met my ex-husband, how it was in the beginning, what was it like raising my kids, why I gave up the corporate world to stay at home, what that looked like, and how I felt. He asked when I knew the marriage was over. That was the tough stuff for me. That was when I had to choose to be vulnerable and authentic. His questions continued … how the separation went, how the divorce was, what did my world look like after the divorce, the first few months up until that moment…. All of those questions were good, went deep, and created an understanding between us. I spoke first, taking the chance to be open and exposed. He followed up with the same degree of vulnerability and honesty, sharing his story with me. And as we reached the top of the mountain, our goal for one way, we also reached the emotional bond that I've been looking for in a man. Connection.

Breathtaking. The view was stunning. Jax pulled out a small blanket from his backpack gear and laid it down. We were alone on top of the world. He helped me sit down. He unpacked treats of hummus with carrots and celery, cheese and crackers, power bars, and vitamin drinks. He was an excellent planner. He must have been out running around that morning thinking about what to bring and getting the items. I loved this about him. He was definitely a romantic, something not necessary, but oh, how good I felt to be the beneficiary. Just for a moment, I thought about how good he, so attentive to details and needs, must be in bed. Giver.

I told him I appreciated his thoughtfulness in planning all this at the last moment. He smiled. He liked the compliments. He sat down next to me after he set up our little picnic in our private world. I was staring out, taking in my yoga deep breaths that offer peace. I wanted to remember the sights, the sounds, the view, the smells, and Jax. All of Jax. We didn't talk. We'd been talking on and off for about two hours, ending with the heavy conversation of our marriages and divorces. He lifted some food up and fed me.

He looked out at the view when I turned to look at him. I thought he was the most beautiful man I'd ever seen, not only physically, but in his soul. I adored him. I leaned over to him while he looked beyond and laid my head on his shoulder. He wrapped his arms around me, holding me close. We spoke no words, but everything was said in that moment of togetherness.

After a while, he put away the items and sat back down behind me. He wrapped his legs around my body, and I leaned back into him as he held me close. We sat there, halfway lying down, for some time. Then he kissed me again on the back of my neck. I melted. I didn't care about holding myself together. I turned around quickly to him. I urgently and intently began to kiss him, first on the mouth, then everywhere—his neck, his ears, in his hair, his collarbone. Then I pulled down his shirt. Then I pulled off his shirt and kissed his chest and his nipples with a soft bite. A nice moan came from him. I continued on his lats, his stomach, his bellybutton. All the way down to his pants. I stopped there.

I lay down on top of him. Kissing me back, he gently flipped me to my side to face him. Now he was aiming to please me. He didn't hold back with his desire. He kissed me deep inside my mouth and moved to all over my neck, ears, and quickly down to my shoulder. He pulled my shirt to the side as he moved along my collarbone, shoulder, and arm. Then he slowed down, moving with intent, enjoying my little jumps every time he hit a new spot. My breath went quicker, letting soft pleasures out of my mouth, allowing my mind to float away.

He kissed then licked me at the base of my throat, slowly moving down the center of my chest, pulling my shirt down with his movements. He licked all the way down to the middle of my breasts and stopped. He went back to kissing one breast and then to the other, kissing only the tops of them and not going any farther. My body was moving. I wanted him badly. But that was all he was going to give me for now.

He moved back up my upper body, kissing every part of it all the way back up to my mouth. He stopped there with a deep long kiss before sitting up, pulling his shirt back on, and then standing. He held his hand out for me to take and stand.

Wow, he is the one who stopped, not me. I thought about that. I would have let him go way farther on my body. I was not sure how to react or respond. I stood and helped him wrap the blanket away. Deep in my thoughts, I asked myself if he had changed his mind about me and decided I wasn't what he wanted. I felt completely exposed, almost embarrassed. Not sure what to say, I remained quiet. I didn't even know how to act. All was packed up, so we both turned for a moment to take in the beautiful views and deep air before we began the descent back down. Jax took two steps in front of me to begin, then turned, smiled, and took my hand. *Okay, maybe he is processing. Maybe he is not sure but doesn't want the day to be ruined. Maybe, maybe, maybe.*

A few moments later, he must have felt my nervous energy because he stopped and turned to me. "Skye, I wanted you very much. But I feel strongly that we should take things slowly. You still have some healing left inside of you that you may or may not be aware of, and I want to make sure we were on equal ground before going farther in our sexual exploration."

I swear to God, my mouth dropped. I was stunned into silence. Was he an Intuitive? Empath? Psychic? I didn't think God created men like that. I am intuitive, self-aware, and empathetic, but I was completely taken aback by his words. Now, it was my turn to process. I couldn't do it quickly enough. I pulled away from his hand, too exposed, suddenly scared. All confidence was gone. I felt sad. I felt tears coming to my eyes, and I hated it. I am not a big crier and prefer to cry alone. I wanted to run back to the parking lot and call an Uber. I wanted to disappear. I had revealed too much to him. My feelings and emotions were too much. *I* was too much.

It is amazing how quickly all of those stories you are told most of your life by people who supposedly love you come running to the forefront when your soul is in your throat. I panicked. I stepped back from him. *Gosh, don't cry, Skye, keep your shit together.* I couldn't look him in the eyes. I just said, "I'm sorry," and started walking away from him down the mountain. I lectured myself in my head, starting the belittling, the typical, *You're not worthy of love, this was too good to be true, you blew it.* Oh, how you beat yourself up so badly, going right down to the core beliefs that society, family, or others place in you before you even know who you are. How the trauma of life appears in seconds when you thought you had dealt with it.

Tears started to flow down my face—not a ton because I was yelling at myself in my head to stop them. Another side of me rose up to tell myself to calm down, this was old stuff, old patterns, and that this didn't mean the truth. I told myself to allow the feelings and let them go. *This too shall pass.* The voice of reason came in at the perfect moment. But the tears still flowed as I felt all the rejection and insecurities that have played in my head for decades. In reality, I knew it wasn't about Jax but myself; however, these situations always come out in any real relationship. Relationships are the truest test of all the work you've done and reveal the work that remains to be done. To go to the next level, you must go through a relationship test. Obviously, I still had work that needed to be done.

Jax came jogging after me. He told me to stop, but I kept going. My pace quickened. Plus, because I was going downhill, moving faster was easier. He caught up and stopped me. He turned me to face him, but I was hiding my face, staring down at the ground. I could not look into his eyes. It was unbearable. I was sure there were streaks of tears running down my face. I grew a determination inside me. *Guard up. Protect.* I decided not to say a word to him. He lifted my chin to see my face, but I averted my eyes to the side so I didn't look at him.

He didn't let me get away with it. He moved his body to my eyes and continued to do so until he asked me to stop looking away. So, I did. I looked at him. But where they had danced before, they now glared, on guard with steely determination. I'd shut him out. He immediately saw it, and I could see he was disappointed or sad. He was about to say something, for his mouth opened, but he stopped himself and instead grabbed and pulled me to him. Making me rest my head on his chest, he held me close. He actually started to rock side to side, with me wrapped up cozily against him. I started to soften. There was something about his presence that soothed me.

After a bit of time, I relaxed, letting go of all those emotions while he held me close. I have no idea how long we stood there doing this small dance between us in silence, but it was more than a few minutes. When he felt me relax, he kissed my forehead. He said, "I'm sorry for what I said. It wasn't my intention to make you feel that way or bring up anything negative. What I really want is for you to be one-hundred percent sure with me so that you don't have any regrets." He didn't want to disappoint me. That brought tears to my eyes again. He had a kind heart. One that cared. I would remember that.

Finally, we started to walk down, but it was different than the way up. On the way down, there was a deepening. We walked very close to each other, in sync like our bodies, minds, and souls were somehow one. It was as if we were a part of each other, twin flames designed to be together but separated at birth only to be joined together again. I'd never felt anything like that in my entire life and truly thought I never would again. If he'd have me, I wouldn't let him go. I needed him in my life. He could take me to places I'd never imagined within myself. I knew it would be painful at times, but I also knew it would be the greatest joy ever experienced.

Listening to silence when no one is talking is a great way to learn about someone. I can talk a lot; however, I can listen well, too. We didn't talk on the way down or in the car. On the way back, I rolled the window down to let the fresh air blow, and I turned up the radio. Neither of us said much at all. A sense of "whatever" attitude had come over me during the ride home. I was not focused on Jax at all. I was in my mind. This is a defense mechanism to avoid rejection and/or abandonment fears that still arise. Mine will be a lifelong process to deal with these core issues.

We arrived at my house. I grabbed my things, and he walked me to the door. I turned to thank him for the day and opened the door. Pepper was dying to go outside and so happy to have me home. She ran outside, jumping all over Jax, and then out to the yard for her business.

As I waited for her, Jax walked into my house. What was he doing? I didn't ask him in or even give a sense of welcoming. I wanted to be alone to take a nap. Napping is a coping mechanism to many of my problems in life. I couldn't say anything without sounding rude, so I walked inside and closed the door. Jax had already made himself at home. He was sitting down on my sofa, like he'd been there or in my space a million times. I offered him some water, got it from the kitchen, and went to sit down in a chair next the sofa. Obviously, he wanted to talk, which was something else I didn't want to do at that moment. He looked at me softly and asked me to sit next to him. Reluctantly, I complied. When I looked him in his eyes, I saw a shift. There was an intensity, a determination, or an obsession.

In that same moment, he grabbed me and started kissing me. Just like I saw a shift in his eyes, I now felt the shift in his body. He was not soft, gentle, or sweet. He was intense, raw, and hungry. He was focused. On what, I didn't know, but I felt his emotions so clearly. His kissing, deeper and more passionate, was meant to get to my soul. Placing his hands around my neck, he swiftly moved there, harder, with more sucking, and my body responded with equal intensity. Whatever I was thinking and feeling was gone. I was now focused on the sensations that this pleasure was bringing me. He pulled my shirt to the side as he moved to my shoulders and tops of my arms. He moved his hands around my waist, pulling me closer to him. I released all of my resolve. I let him lead. I complied to his needs. I surrendered to whatever was coming. Then he stood, fast. Once again, I thought he wanted to stop, and the insecure feelings in me started to arise. But this time, when he stood, he grabbed my hands and pulled me up to him. He placed his hands around my hips and started to literally move my body, like a dancer, closer to my bedroom.

There were no words. Only eye contact, physical movement, and kissing. A step back in one direction, a kiss on the neck. Another step, a kiss on the shoulder, a few more steps, deep in the mouth, dancing all the way to the bed. He sat me down on the edge of the bed. He stood above me at first, and then he went all the way down to his knees in front of me.

When he did this, a part of me was thrilled with excitement, and the other part was scared to death. I hadn't been with a man since the divorce. And it was daytime. I was fully exposed, I would have to show my body when I preferred darkness and covers, especially for the first time. Somehow, I knew he was not thinking like that, but women, we do.

Once on his knees in front of me, he pulled me by my hips close to the edge of the bed. He leaned up to continue the kissing. As he moved to my other shoulder, he again pulled my shirt to the side. He then took his hand and pulled my shirt off. Quickly, efficiently, I complied. He moved down to the center of my breasts to kiss, suck, and lick above them but not under the bra. He didn't touch my breasts. He gently laid my body down on my back on top of the bed as he moved on top hovering over me. His upper body wasn't touching mine. He was like a plank above me, he kissed down to my stomach. He slowed down. New territory. He went back to kissing my mouth gently, taking it in, turning me partially sideways to then lick all the way down my flanks. My body shuddered.

I was on my back again, and he kissed my stomach, licking and sucking everywhere. Licking the belly button and down to the top of my pants, he slowed down. He moved out of plank position and leaned his full body into mine. He was an expert kisser. He kissed all around the top of my pants, pulling them back slightly to get more access. Teasing, he kissed there, pulled up, kissed my mouth, lowered down, moved to the next spot, then stopped. The sensations were out of this world. Over to the hips, which are such a sensitive area on top of the hip bone, he sucked hard, grabbing his hands around my hips and butt, pulling me up ever so slightly, then down again. He was a giver. I let out a moan. I was wet. Up again he came to my face. He told me to open my eyes as he looked lovingly into my soul. He leaned all the way down on top of me to kiss my mouth, deeply, again.

As the sexual tension continued, he took his entire body and wrapped it around mine. His hands were moving everywhere all over me. Up my back, down my back, around my stomach, hips, legs, shoulders. He moved me every way he wished. Our bodies were full on touching. So intense, so intimate.

He was generous. My breathing was shallow, my body wanted more, and I no longer cared that it was daylight. He made me forget about the world, my mind, my flaws and insecurities, and only think of the present moment where I was lustfully wanted.

He sat up for a second to take off his shirt. He was well built. He had a medium size build with strong arms, and surprisingly, given his age, a pretty toned stomach. In no way did he have ripped abs, but he also didn't have the beer gut that so many men have. He looked great. Some chest hair, but not hairy. I leaned up to kiss him, to give to him, but he said no and pushed me gently back down on to the bed. He wanted to lead. Back down on top of me, he rolled me with him to the side. Quickly, the bra came off and he was pressing his body into mine. Not rushing, not looking, but feeling my skin against his while kissing me. He let out a moan.

With our bodies tightly wound together, I felt him so hard. My wetness increased. My tits became hard. As he became more generous, I became greedier. I wanted more. I didn't know what it was about him, but it was almost like he knew what I needed in order to feel safe. With all that he did, he continued to make me feel protected. He did not rush or jump ahead. He took his time, giving me the space to relax and get out of my head. He paused for a moment, came up for air, and took a deep breath. Then he looked me straight into my eyes. His stare was serious and kind. That moment, I saw right into his soul. I could see his beauty, his open heart, and the light inside him.

He spoke for the first time, "Skye, I want you so much, you have no idea; however, I promised you that today I would not make love to you. It's too soon, and I want to explore all of you first."

He had set a boundary. I felt more comfortable, knowing that what came next would not lead to sex, and that made me feel safe. I was not ready for the whole process yet. He sensed this about me. It was uncanny how he could almost read my mind and respond so emotionally connected. Rare.

I felt myself loosening up. He held tight, slowly moving his hands up and down my back. He kissed from my mouth straight down to the center of my breasts. Holding me tightly to him as he progressed, he started gently kissing each of my breasts, going back and forth between them. It had been a while for me, so the feeling was powerful. He sucked my nipples, grabbed them strongly, and ended with small bites. That's when I lost myself in my fantasy world. He flipped me on my back as he planked over me again, proceeding down to the edge of my pants. At this point, he began to take my pants off, slowly pulling them down, while kissing all of me step by step. My body tensed awake. Once they were off, he stood and took his pants off, both of us still wearing underwear. Then he began again, at my feet. He licked the top of my foot, up the calf, and grabbed my inner thighs. I gasped with delight.

He moved my body closer to the edge of the bed, kissing my inner thighs while grabbing them, holding tight. His hands moved to the top of my hips as he slyly took off my underwear. Again, he pulled me closer to the edge, to him. At this moment, he came all the way back up to my face and kissed me passionately.

Then he asked, "Are you okay?"

What man does that? What man checks on you during a full body exploration. I was more than okay, and I let him know. In fact, I could not wait. All the way back down he went, onto his knees at the edge of the bed. My entire lower body was throbbing. He took each of my legs and wrapped them around his neck. A strong pull on my hips had me hanging slightly off the bed. Again, his hands grabbed around my legs as he began to suck strongly on my inner thighs, inching ever so slightly up to my succulent cherry.

The first kiss he gave to my love box caused my body to reactively arch up. I could almost see him smiling as he proceeded to give kissing sensations all around before going in for the clit. Oh my gosh, it felt so good. I felt such a wet gush as my body responded as it should. This was something else I worried about … how my body would respond. Nicely, everything reacted appropriately. He kissed my clit, slowly beginning to suck, gently moving and taking it all in while his hands grabbed me around my hips and then my butt, pulling and stirring me in a sexual motion while he continued to give to me generously. The sensations were so strong in me that I finally begin to leave my mind, going into the fantasy world I could live in so often. I enjoyed every second and let go.

Every so often, he stopped and placed his entire face into my succulent pie, smelling me, then back to tasting, sucking, kissing. Around and around, I could not help the moans and sounds of pleasure coming out of my mouth. That went on for a while. He was very patient … very good with the tongue … he knew what he was doing. As I slipped deeper into ecstasy while responding with my body, he once again surprised me by adding his finger. Now, my body completely jolted. One, two, three fingers went in while he continued to suck and kiss my clit.

His fingers explored slowly at first and in the same rhythm as his mouth. My body reacted like crazy, moving, not able to stay still. I can't describe the sounds coming out of my throat. He placed his other hand, the one that wasn't inside me, on top of my lower stomach and pushed down. He was holding me in place. Then his fingers inside me started to move with more purpose. He went quicker, reaching up and curling to hit my g-spot. A sensation came over me while he was still moving purposely on my clit and holding me down. Faster, harder. Wetness was pouring out of me as my breath became short. Sometimes I hold my breath for more intensity. Thank you, yoga, for teaching me how to control my breathing. I was getting close. I grabbed the sides of my bed with fists. I told him, "I'm close."

He moved faster, harder, and removed his mouth while placing the hand that was holding me down on top of the clit. He pushed down hard, rubbing hard. One hand with fingers inside while the other pressing down hard and moving on top of the clit. This did it for me. Within a minute, my body and mind exploded in orgasm.

I let my voice go, loudly moaning with the release of pleasure. I squirmed like crazy, eventually sitting straight up as my body hit the peak of sexual pleasure. Jax moved with me, slowing down but not stopping. When I climaxed and sat up, I opened my eyes to see Jax was literally staring right at me. Our eyes locked as my body started to calm down. He was smirking. He slowly released his hands from on top, then inside as he moved down to taste all the juices flowing like a river out of me. My entire pussy was still quaking from the intense orgasm. After he delighted in his satisfaction, he climbed his way on top of me.

Trying to catch my breath, I fell back. He lay on his side next me, watching my breath slowly return to normal. I wanted to go to sleep. Suddenly tired, I closed my eyes. I knew that for him to give so generously to me, I would return the favor to him. He was up next. He wrapped himself around me just like the beginning. His legs around mine, he pulled me to the side with him, pressing his body tightly around me. He started to whisper to me while I was still recovering.

He said, "You are so beautiful and exquisite. You turn me on so much, and it's very hard not to take all of you at once. I want to please you. I enjoy your body and sounds. You fit perfectly with my body. I want more of you. This won't even begin to be the last time."

I locked my eyes into his to see if he was sincere or playing with me. When I can remove the logic in my mind and go completely with my heart, I am usually right. Looking into his soul through his eyes, I believed he was sincere. I felt wanted, appreciated, and fulfilled. All those other guys, the players, the liars, just want to take not give, and they make a woman feel cheap and used afterwards. This switches off her emotional feelings and places sex into a logical place. Then, the woman begins to use sex only as a physical pleasure and not an emotional connection. This allows the woman to rationalize sex objectively, as a means to an end. I am all feelings and emotions. I am all about connection. I desire more from a sexual partner.

I turned to my sexual partner, for I had waited for this and wanted Jax to be that for me. There was zero doubt in my mind. I kissed him deeply and slowly, for my heart was open and free. I said, "It's your turn."

As I was about to begin taking my time with him, he stopped me. Saying, "No, this was about you, not me. My time will come very soon. I want you to relish in the pleasure, relax in your mind and body, and relive each moment that gave you such joy."

I was stunned. Never, ever, would I have imagined a man saying that to me. His emotional IQ was off the charts. I asked him if he was sure because I told him I wanted to please him. He said he was sure. He held me close, and I still felt him rock hard. What self-control he had, and I fell fast asleep in his arms, my body and mind completely content, safe, and protected.

When I woke, Jax wasn't with me in bed. Quickly, I looked at the clock. It was 7:00 PM. I had been asleep for two hours. I'd never sleep that night since I already had issues in that department. I wondered if he'd left, not knowing what he had planned. We really never got to that discussion. But as I pulled myself out of the deep slumber and hit the bathroom, I heard someone in my kitchen. I threw water on my face, brushed my teeth, and got dressed. I came out of the bedroom to see Jax cooking something up. *Nice, he cooks.* This is another trait I was very unaccustomed to in a man. And he didn't leave. I peeked around the corner, slyly wanting to watch him. He sensed my presence. He smiled first before even looking at me. He said, "Hi sexy sleepy head. How are you feeling?"

I smiled back, already wanting him again. I believed in being as authentic and honest as possible, not playing head games, so I answered him frankly by stating I felt completely content and fulfilled. He looked surprised, with his eyebrows raised and a sexy smirk on his lips. I knew he loved my answer.

I walked over to him and wrapped my arms around his waist as he was cooking. He turned the stove top off and pushed me against the other side of the counter. Moving a strand of hair away from my face, he placed his hands around my face, looked at me tenderly in the eyes, and kissed me passionately. I lusted for him immensely. With the self-control that he had (something I'd need to work toward), he said it was time for dinner. He'd made himself perfectly at home in my place. Grabbing dishes and silverware while pouring a great meal on the plate, we worked together to sit down. I didn't cook much, so I was surprised there was real food around. He managed to make a ground turkey dish with fresh vegetables and a pesto tomato sauce. It was delicious, and I realized I was famished.

55

We sat at the kitchen table and ate with big smiles on our faces. It was like we were kids who had a secret together. After we ate, we both cleaned up the dishes together. That was also nice. Together, when I thought of a partner, these were the daily joys I wanted to have.

I said, "I need to take the dog for a quick walk."

He said, "I'd love to go with you."

Like a married couple, we walked the dog together out in the open so all my nosy neighbors could see. Oh, well. I'd been divorced long enough; they could see a man at my place. After we returned, I asked him what his week looked like, for the next day was a workday. He told me about some project coming up and what that entailed. I wondered if he was going to be leaving soon.

Instead of parting ways, he directly asked if he could stay until morning. No man had slept in my bed. In fact, I hadn't had a man in my place for longer than two hours at one time. I protected my privacy and space. I cherish my alone time, especially in the mornings, but this man was giving me everything I'd been dreaming of. I really didn't want him to leave.

I said, "Of course you can stay."

I also told him that I have weird sleep issues and might be up really early. I asked him if he wanted coffee in the morning and what I should do if I wake up because I didn't want to disrupt his sleep. He asked what I usually do, so I shared my weirdness. He laughed, because yes, I have some quirky habits, and said for me to do my thing. It wouldn't disrupt him at all. I was relieved that I didn't need to change my morning routine.

But the night was still young. We sat down on the couch and just started talking. Instead of talking about our past, since we'd covered most of that earlier that day, he started asking me about what I'm looking for in a relationship. I hesitated because I didn't want to ask for things that may be out of reach or traits he may doubt in himself. Plus, I didn't know where he stood. So I suggested, "Like today, if I say something, you have to say something, too. That way neither of us is in a freefall of talking about relationships. We can think about what we will say next while still listening to the other." He smiled. Either he enjoyed my thought process, or he realized what I was thinking. So, I began.

Nearly two hours later, we concluded the discussion. What I was most happy about was how much we truly wanted the same things. Our morals and values naturally aligned. He wanted a committed, monogamous, relationship but not a marriage at this time. The top five things we looked for matched. It was amazing to me how much we agreed and how similar our outlooks were. It all felt easy and natural. Those were the tests we gave each other to see if something could hold, withstand outside pressure, and align as a couple while we could still be ourselves. That is what I like to call co-independent. It is imperative to me to have a healthy, loving, and trusting partner. I didn't want to worry when he traveled that he was with someone else (or even looked at someone else). I didn't want to ask him to call or text me and touch base daily. I didn't want to wait for him or his life. I wanted to live my life and for him to live his while coming together in full partnership of trust, honesty, and love.

His Turn

Soon, I was finished talking for the day and my lust reappeared. I took his hand and led him into the bedroom. Earlier, I worried about my body and all those insecurities. Those doubts were gone. He had seen, felt, smelled, and tasted me everywhere. He enjoyed every aspect of me, so there was no hiding, which freed me completely. Confidence came. It was rewarding. It was my turn to please him. I took control. I laid him down on the bed and mounted him.

He was smirking, which only turned me on more. I kissed him zealously. I started kissing him all over his neck, ears, and chest. I quickly removed his shirt. I touched his chest, stomach, and arms, and kissed, sucked, and moved. I felt his hardness. I wanted to go there, but I reminded myself to take time like he had with me. There should be no rush at this stage. He allowed me to seduce him. I took off his pants, leaving his underwear, and threw my clothes off as well, leaving my bra and underwear on. It was too tempting for me to be completely naked.

I took my time kissing, exploring, feeling, smelling him from top to bottom without going near his package. The entire process turned me on so much, and I was unbelievably wet. Several times, he grabbed me and wrapped himself around me to kiss. He liked to communicate but not too much, saying sweet words like, "Sexy, driving me wild, more here, beautiful…" He was hard to resist. Finally, I touched him, gently at first and through the cloth of his underwear. Quickly, though, I went down to my knees as I pulled them off. Now it was his turn to moan and let the sweet sounds of pleasure be released.

He was a perfect size for me—well above average, but not so big that I was scared. He was manscaped which is thoughtful, sexy, and necessary. I smiled to myself. I was going to enjoy this. I grabbed his inner thighs, listened as a moan released, and moved up to take his balls in my mouth. Sucking ever so gently, I moved back to his inner thighs. I licked his perineum. I came up and grabbed his hands and sucked on his fingers while he took my fingers into his mouth. I moved down again, biting gently on his nipples, licking toward the top of his penis. Slowly, I took his package into my mouth.

His body jerked. I went slowly, for I needed to see how deep I could take him. I could go almost all the way. I came back up, released him, and started licking him all around his shaft, moving my hand down to his balls and grabbing his thighs hard. I kissed him below the top of his penis head, a very sensitive spot on a man, and his body jerked again. Then, when I knew he was fully turned on, I went down on him completely. Sucking, licking, taking him all into my mouth, I used my hands to touch him below his penis, grab his hips, and push and pull him at my control. All the while, sucking on him, slowly at first, teasing, releasing, plunging down, then tighter, harder, a bit quicker. He grabbed my hair. He was moaning like crazy.

I went deeper. He told me he was close. I slowed down for a moment, to build the momentum, then went deep and quick so he could come. And when he did come, it was an explosion. He let out an animalistic sound from deep within his body. I slowed way down on him, taking in his juices, swallowing most of it, and then I took some of his cum on my hand and rubbed it into my pussy, which was swelling with anticipation with a quick touch from me. As his body started to relax, I decided to finish with a quick and light licking on his cock head. It drove him wild. Then I kissed it and moved up to his face. He grabbed me hard, flipping me onto my back. I felt his heart beating so fast. His eyes had a cloudy look. He lay on top of me, kissing my face. He placed his head on my chest.

He held me tight and relaxed. I kissed the top of his head and slowly rubbed my hands through his hair as I allowed his body to return to a normal pace. Then I was the one smirking.

More

Well, so much for me holding out. In one weekend filled with almost non-stop togetherness, I gave him all of me except the full-on deed. That included the mental, emotional, and vulnerable parts to me as well. However, I felt that he met me in the same spaces. We were on equal ground. My intuition said he was not going to leave me high and dry. We would see. I can be gullible, so being taken advantage of, well, let's just say it wouldn't have been the first time. But in that moment, I was happy. I sat in it, relishing the feelings and letting go of what was ahead. I grew tired. My clock read 1:00 AM, and I needed sleep.

Gently, I moved to let Jax know I wanted to get up. He released me as I went to get ready for bed. It was weird to have someone in my bed. I had grown accustomed to being alone. After a few moments, Jax was in my bathroom with me. He asked if I had a toothbrush to spare, which I did. I threw on a nightgown, let Pepper up on the bed, hoping he didn't mind that she sleeps with me, and crawled under the covers. He turned off the light in the bathroom and went to the other side of the bed to enter. He moved Pepper to the bottom of the bed instead of the middle of it. She complied. He came over to me, turned me to face him, gently kissed me, thanked me for an amazing weekend, then said, "Goodnight sexy."

Normally, I like to sleep without touching, but that night I wrapped myself into him and his arms as we fell fast asleep. I woke up around 5:00 AM still entangled with him. A deep sensation of desire filled me as I felt Jax's body, steadily breathing, and stared at his handsome looks. Instead of going about my usual morning routine, I allowed myself to focus on what I wanted. I started kissing his body and moving my hands lightly all around him. With only an hour before he had to leave, I had to be greedy. He awakened, and

I knew that because I saw his cock hard. Then he gently grabbed my hair, pulling me up to his face for the deep kiss we both loved. His kiss alone could arouse me to new heights. Yesterday, we had all the time in the world, but this morning we were limited. I lifted from our deep kiss to say, "We only have an hour."

Other than that, no words were spoken. We were all action. The slow, exploratory phase of yesterday was gone and replaced by a craving. Grabbing me hard, he quickly put me on my back. The long, slow kisses were replaced by raw lust. There was nothing slow or gentle anymore. He sucked me all over, bit my breasts, and moved his hands hard all over. Instantly I was aroused. He reached up to kiss me deeply and bit my lips while simultaneously putting his fingers in my wet slit. I moaned loudly. His fingers went deep inside me hard and fast. I opened my eyes because I wanted to look at him.

My hands pulled him close to my body, grabbing his back, gyrating together like full on sex. The movement alone created more sexual tension in me. I started to bite him, licked his face, grabbed his hair, and pulled him closer. The sensation of wanting him inside me was overwhelming. We stared into each other's eyes. He let out a moan and then began to manhandle me. He pulled his fingers out of me, grabbed my hips, and pulled me down low on the bed. He flipped me over on my stomach. Then he was kissing and licking my back as his fingers went back into me. All the way down he went to my booty, and trust me, I have one. He started licking, sucking, and biting hard all over my ass. His other hand wrapped around my waist, and he pulled, pushed, and moved me to his liking. He was in total control of my body. Fingering me hard, biting my ass, moving me to his desires. The feelings were sensational. I reached down on myself to press into my clit, stimulating myself to get the full effect, getting close to exploding. He must have known I was close and was not ready to give me the pleasure, for he quickly flipped me again and pulled me lower still. Then he mounted on top of me backward.

Then, his face planted into my fire pit. With his fingers back inside my, he placed his other hand behind my back and pulled me up to him. I was very aware of his hard package immediately in front of my face. I reached up behind his butt and pulled him hard into my mouth. I loved his dick. I tasted it, licked it, and sucked hard. This was not a gentle morning. It aroused me more. Within moments, I was climaxing. Pausing on him as my body released, I cried out in pleasure.

As soon as the moment passed and he was still absorbing me, I went back to him with great energy to ensure he was as well pleased as I was. Everything was so easy with our bodies. They played well together. Nothing awkward, no extra maneuvering, we were a natural fit.

He rolled off of me and we lay side by side in opposite directions. He took my hand and held it next to him as we both slowly came down from our heights. I couldn't remember the last time I had done a sixty-nine but wondered why I hadn't done it more. That was one of the many benefits of starting over again later in life—exploration, excitement, and adventure.

Jax got up. He needed to leave. He went into the kitchen to get himself some coffee, asked what I took in mine (cream), and brought me back a cup. He gave me a kiss on the lips and said, "Well that was a great morning start, beautiful." Then he set the coffee down next to the bed. He went into the bathroom to get dressed. I took a smiling sip and grabbed my computer to start my day. When he came out, he sat on the edge of the bed. I gave him my attention because he was about to leave.

Jax said, "Clearly it has been an amazing weekend with you. And I intend for it to be the beginning of many. I'm not traveling this week and would like to see you again. Can we set a date to get together?"

I looked at my schedule and said, "How does Thursday work?"

He didn't even look at his calendar and said, "Perfect." He was making me a priority. As he stood to leave, he held his hand out, so I took it and got up. I grabbed my nightgown from the floor, threw it on, and walked him to the door. Before he left, Jax turned to me, staring me down with those intense eyes. He kissed me deeply and said, "See you soon, sexy." After a tight hug, he walked out the door. I watched him. I observed his walk and his body. Then he turned before getting into his car and gave me a wink and a huge smile. Charming.

Thrilled

Over the next few days, all I did was replay our time together, especially the complete satisfaction I had enjoyed from Jax. Why do we women do this to ourselves—thinking, analyzing, replaying each scene with an obsessive viewpoint? I questioned, *What could I have said differently, and what could I have done better?* We over think. I believe men just go about their business and don't think too much about anything beyond the physical and emotional pleasure.

I will say that I was impressed with Jax. He texted me every morning, since he knew I was always up early. He called every night just to check in on my day, and we talked for an hour each time, getting to know each other better. He sent me a huge bouquet of two dozen red roses overflowing in a gorgeous vase with a deep message, "Beautiful Skye, you are not someone I will find twice." Interested.

I was thrilled to be chased and not left high and dry. That was a huge relief for me. There are many dates, many chances, many toads in the world, but I'd worked on my energy vibration level to get high enough to bring someone in who was exactly like Jax. The wait was completely worth it at every level for me. While I put myself back out in the world, taking risks and pushing out of my comfort zones, I continued to grow and learn. I worked deeper on my issues, and it was important for me to keep moving forward and become the best version of myself. My plan is to continue this process for the rest of my life, so it is imperative that I find someone who aspires to grow and will do the work with me.

When Jax and I talked, our conversations were a meeting of two minds. He was similar to me in his thought process, yet our journeys had been different. I heard him and tried to fully understand his path, which helped me to grow and learn in my own way.

Sometimes, it was uncanny how similar we were; I was looking in a mirror at a male me.

Thursday arrived. Anticipating like a little girl, I walked on air all day. Jax texted me that morning and said he was picking me up at 6:30 PM and to wear an elegant dress. Great, I was glad he told me what to wear so I didn't have to ask a million questions. Again, he'd already picked up on some of my rational needs, and he'd answered them ahead of time. Of course, he didn't say where we were going; however, I like happy surprises and assumed dinner was involved. For tonight, I wanted to look sexy for him. I wanted him to unleash his desires upon me. I picked a form-fitting, black, halter dress that showed my breasts off nicely while fitting perfectly on my hip bones. It landed at the top of my knees. I grabbed my Karl Lagerfeld, three-inch, black heels and prayed I didn't faceplant. I packed my small, Gucci, black bag and was ready to go.

Of course, he was right on time to pick me up. He wore a big smile, and my entire body flooded with heightened awareness. I opened the door and he stopped for a moment to say, "Wow, you look stunning." He stepped inside and as I closed the door, he grabbed my waist, pulling me into him with a fiery, deep, long kiss. Coming up for air, I grabbed his face and greedily went for more kissing. I never wanted to stop kissing this man. Ever. With his proven self-control, he said we needed to go.

Grabbing my hand, helping me down the stairs, and opening the car door, he knew how to make a woman feel like a lady. On the way, he talked about how much he missed me, how every time he saw me I became more beautiful, and about the emotions he felt when he saw me. What man talks like that?

We'd covered the "how's the week" and "work issues" by talking every day, so small talk was quickly over between us. While he talked, I fantasized, listening to but also looking at him while he drove. He was wearing a long-sleeved, fitted, button-down shirt with cool looking jeans, a brown belt, and leather shoes. He was stylish but didn't look like he was trying. I stared at his profile. His features were sweet to my eyes. He had gorgeous skin color that women would die for and a touch of stubble all around. After admiring his looks and style, I could only think about going down on him right then in his sexy car. *Where do such thoughts even come from? What am I, in high school?* I looked straight ahead to calm my panties down.

I enjoyed that he liked to talk when he was in the car. I preferred to remain quiet. I was along for the ride. He pulled into the St. Regis Hotel. I'd been there plenty before for the bar scene. The beautiful venue is one of the best pick up places in Atlanta for forty-plus divorcees and singles. He valeted the car and held my hand as we strolled into the place. We slowly walked together, taking our time, having not a care in the world until we got to The Garden Room dining establishment. It's such a romantic place for dinner. We sat in a corner. I could only assume he had asked for a more private table, because it was almost like we were by ourselves. The chairs were literally side by side. As soon as we sat, his hand was on my leg, and he leaned in close to me to talk. His eyes were so intense, like he was staring into my soul. I felt mine melting when I looked at him. I knew that we would talk in depth tonight by the way he was looking at me. He was curious to know more.

There was something special about Jax. There was something special about *us*. Our bodies moved together almost like two sources of water flowing into one. We touched each other constantly. We finish each other's sentences. We thought alike. Our conversations could be light or downright intense, all the while feeling completely natural. We seemed to sense each other's emotions and meet each other where he or she was. There was an openness, generosity, and warmth that streamed between our aura energies. We melded together yet could move apart while still feeling a connection no matter how far the distance. All it took was a little tug to bring us back together as one unit.

We both were good talkers and great listeners. There was an innate sense of trust. With Jax, I felt valued, heard, understood, cherished, desired, and feminine. This magic combination is how I fall in love. I wondered what combination could make him fall in love.

Back home, he came in without being asked. It was already late for a weeknight for mid-life people who had to work in the morning. I was waiting to be attacked … wanting to be. Jax was far more casual on this front. He asked "Alexis" to play a certain station. It was gentle, relaxing music. He grabbed my hand to pull me toward him and started to sway. I wrapped my hands around his neck and let them fall casually. He pressed my body tightly into him, but he kept my face in front of his. After a few minutes, I wrapped my arms around his waist and laid my face down on his chest sideways like I had the very first time I met him. I closed my eyes, absorbing all the energy between us. And we danced, slowly blending into one.

I was relaxed in his strong arms and felt a sense of peace while we danced. He soon reached down to lift my head and softly kiss me. He was in a calm, loving mood. Kissing is so underrated. A brush on the lips led to soft brushes on the face. Swaying, dancing, kissing. He kissed my cheeks, nose, forehead, the tops of my closed eyes, chin, back to the lips, into my mouth. He told "Alexis" to play U2's "All I Want Is You" on repeat.

As he held me to him, I leaned my head back so he could move to my neck. Soft, buttery kisses landed down the sides of my throat. Taking his time, pausing, absorbing, he blended into me. He unzipped the back of my dress, and it fell to the ground as we continued to move like a flowing river. I had on a black silk slip under the dress. We danced in front of my large mirror hanging in the family room, and he turned me around to face it.

Standing behind me, swaying, holding me around my waist, I watched him take me in. For just one moment, he looked up so I could meet his eyes in the mirror with that smirk of his before he moved my hair to the side and kissed the nape of my neck. His hands glided around my waist, feeling the silk on me. I watched in the mirror. My body became hot as he activated my senses. Moving to my shoulder, kissing it, he glanced up, staring intently into my eyes in the mirror. Taking one strap off my arm while kissing, never stopping his attention, he watched as half the slip fell to my hip and exposed one breast and half my body. I felt long, sweeping kisses down my arm. Watching, swaying, moving to the music, he bent as I placed my exposed arm on his back. He kissed my flanks from the tops of my hips up to my armpits. My mouth gaped open, and I stopped dancing, but he was not having that, so he moved his hands to my hips and continued to sway me while kissing. Then he was standing tall next to me and sideways. I never took my eyes off the mirror.

I watched his reflection. He stared right at me, obviously feeling the sexual tension and desire rising in both of us. He reached his arms around me from the side as he kissed my collarbone, moving into my upper chest, and back down to my breast. Once there, never taking his mouth off my breast, he glanced up into the mirror to make sure I was watching him. I couldn't take my eyes away. He kissed around the breast, and my nipples became rock hard as chills ran throughout my body. I moaned. I grabbed his head to pull him into me. He pushed my hands back to my sides. He wanted control. Again, I allowed this.

He rose and moved to the back of me, kissing and moving down my half-exposed back. Pulling me from my waist, he controlled my body movement with his hands. Up the center of my back to the back of the neck again. He paused, standing directly behind me. While staring intensely into my eyes through the mirror, he slipped the other side of my dress off, so I was fully exposed in the front. Moving to that side, he began again with the kissing. I watched him intensely, feeling like he was a lion about to mount his mate. He didn't deprive that side, giving it equal time and opportunity. Moving behind me to continue kissing my back, he pulled the slip all the way down. He picked up my leg to lift it out of the slip and removed my shoes as well. I had nothing on but a thong. I watched Jax and myself in the mirror.

On his knees behind me, he grabbed my hips and moved me into his mouth, starting with my derriere. He kissed down the back of my legs, and then licking turned to sucking. He slowly pulled down my thong. I was fully exposed. I was naked in the mirror. He moved on his knees to my side, kissing the sides of my hip, brushing his lips against the lower part of my stomach, putting his hands on my thighs and ass, and moving me into him as I watched.

He stood. He quickly ripped his shirt off and pulled down his pants, leaving his underwear on. He was fully erect. Standing next to me again, this time on the other side, he stared into my soul. I thought, *I'd give everything to know what he's thinking.* He took his right hand and moved it to the front of my face, running a thin, feathery soft line down the center of my body directly to my love spot and stopped. He placed his entire hand on top of my pelvic bone, resting it there, feeling my heat, making me wait. I wished the entire event could be videotaped so I could watch it over and over.

He took one step directly in front of me, taking my stare away from the mirror and directly into his eyes. He leaned down to kiss me deeply and without a touch other than his hand resting on my pelvic bone. Slowly, as his eyes gazed into mine, he bent down to his knees directly in front of me, never taking his eyes away from mine. I know my eyes were glazed. I felt high.

He paused in front of my kitty kat, still meeting my eyes, and told me to watch in the mirror. I looked up. Standing completely naked in front of a mirror with the back of a man's head, a man kneeling in front of me for the first time in a very long time, I felt completely empowered as a woman. In that moment of thought, Jax opened my legs to hip width, moved his mouth on top of my clit, placed his hands on my hips to move me, and began to suck. My body quivered. How sexy it was to watch him go down on me.

Jax's sexual movements made me weak. He started kissing my kitty and then began sucking gently as he moved in sweet circles to create more wetness than was already there. He took his hand and pressed down on top of my love box while simultaneously sucking me. His hand moved down, and his fingers went inside me. I quivered so much I didn't know if I could remain standing. I placed my hands on his shoulders to lean and balance. I watched in the mirror. He took one of my legs and placed it over his shoulder. It rested on the other side of him. His mouth and fingers went deeper into me. There was a table in front of the mirror that I grasped for to hold myself. Animalistic sounds came out of me, deep and raw, like a tiger in the wild. I watched. I felt powerful. I felt free. I felt crazy in the head. I felt everything. I let go. I surrendered to him. As I came, I roared, releasing something deep and wild within me that had been waiting to come out. Still quivering, I collapsed into him on the floor. He caught me and held me close. I couldn't talk, I couldn't catch my breath, I felt insane, and I felt madly in love. And the song repeated. Sensual.

Sensational

In the following days, I stared into that mirror several times a day, reenacting the scene in my mind. Sensations flooded over me every time. Jax and I talked and texted multiple times each day. We grew closer and more intimate in our togetherness. He made future plans with me. He was about to travel for work and asked me to go with him to Mexico. He was going for a couple days for work but wanted to add on the weekend for us. This was a huge move on his part and a big decision for me.

I ran through scenarios. I also knew what a weekend away meant. In my mind, I was all in, however, my hesitation with him was that we were not exclusive. I had not seen anyone else during these two weeks, but we hadn't had the conversation. In reality, he could be seeing other women. I'd been told over and over that the conversation must be had and that one cannot assume. I knew who I was, and to be authentic to myself, I admitted I wanted exclusivity with Jax. I had no idea how to approach the topic because I knew insecurities would arise. What if he didn't want that? What if I scared him off because of it? Was it too soon? Would I seem too serious? Did he have commitment issues?

Like me, Jax was a free spirit; however, unlike me, he had not been domesticated and somewhat tamed through the years. He was like water. Sometimes he was still and peaceful, and at times he flowed freely, moving with dynamics of life. Water can be fun, with splashing and playing, and it can be turbulent, rising up, overtaking you, drowning you. It purifies and heals but can also suffocate. By looking into water, you usually cannot see its depths, which is why you must walk in slowly to feel your way to the deepest parts. On the surface, it may look calm, but underneath it can have riptides ready to toss you around and pull you under.

The debate continued in my head, and I reminded myself that I didn't need to make the decision immediately. He asked to see me that weekend, but already having plans on my calendar, I couldn't see him until Sunday night. I thought about how it was only one night before a weekend away. If I did go, this was twenty-four hours a day for three days of complete togetherness, a.k.a., the works. It was a lot for me to handle so early on. It could be a total disaster, too rushed, or it could be wonderful. I could fall hard. Feelings could be mutual or not. And if they were not, would my heart break? Was I truly ready? Would I jump headfirst into the water?

Sunday night arrived. It had been a minute since we had last seen each other. He had let me know to dress casually. The moment I saw him, a rush and a blush appeared on my face and body. To say the least, the man turned me on. I wanted to run outside and jump into his arms, knocking him off his feet so I could kiss him everywhere. Instead, I waited for him to come in. He led with a huge smile, took quick steps inside the door, grabbing me around the waist, pulled me right into his body, and sincerely kissed me. There had been a longing for both of us.

Normally, at about this time, with his self-control, he would say it was time to go, but that night, he pushed me up against the wall as a look came across his eyes. I hadn't seen the look before. He stared right into me, took a deep breath, (it appeared he was trying to control himself), and attacked my body. His hands were everywhere, feeling, grabbing, like he couldn't take me in enough. He was so far down my throat with his tongue, I could barely catch my breath. He picked me up as I wrapped my legs around him, squeezing me so tightly it took my breath away for a moment. As I adjusted quickly to this new intensity, I tried to meet him exactly where he was and gave him what he wanted. Devouring.

I went into intense mode as well, kissing hard, pulling at his hair, grabbing his body, running my nails down his back, and pushing skin against his. He moved us to the couch, and with me still attached to him, we landed hard on the cushions. Fully clothed, gyrating began, he pushed my hands back trying to take the lead, but I didn't let him. I pushed back. He looked a little surprised, and then the smirk appeared, for he apparently liked this new side of me. He was too intense for me to give him control right then. I wanted to meet him as an equal. He pulled; I pushed. He pushed; I pulled. We moved with obsession. We fell off the couch and on the floor. It was almost like wrestling. He wrapped his legs hard around mine, I pulled away, he grabbed my waist up, and I pushed down. Whatever he did, I did the opposite. He was getting frustrated. I was getting in his head.

For a brief moment, he stopped, got on his knees, ripped off my skirt and underwear and pulled down his pants. He started to jack off right on top of me. Without warning, he plunged his fingers right into me. I was startled and my body was shocked, but only for a second as I was thoroughly enjoying this as much as he was. We climaxed at the same time. He shot his love juice all over my stomach, moving up to my breasts. I took his wad and lotioned my body with it. I put a sweet helping in my mouth for taste.

He grabbed a towel and cleaned me up. I was smiling from ear to ear, and so was he, though not a word was spoken between us. Quickly, we both got dressed. My makeup was smeared all over my face and my hair was a bird's nest, so a quick, ten-minute freshen up was necessary. As we were leaving, he gave me a quick kiss on the lips. Like usual, he talked on the way.

We were going to Punchline Comedy Club to see a guy he loved. I love comedy. More than anything in life, I love to laugh. A few times during the show I noticed Jax observing me. At one point, I laughed so hard I was in tears. I went all in without holding back, which meant I could be loud and dramatic without being self-conscious. I'd glance at him, and he'd be all smiles with those

74

dancing eyes. On the way home, he let me know that he loved seeing me laugh. Seeing me happy made him feel content. He aimed to please.

Back at my place, he asked me if I'd made a decision about Mexico. I hesitated because I hadn't. He immediately picked up on my hesitation. Again, his emotional intelligence was uncanny. We talked about it. He wanted to know what had been holding me back. I grew shy. This was when I should have been direct and asked him about exclusivity, but I still didn't feel confident enough in "us." Instead of being straight with him, I beat around the bush. I said things like it was an entire weekend non-stop together, which was a lot of time, what would happen if we decided it was not what we wanted, and all of those silly other points. He was patient and answered all my doubts and tried to reassure me. There was nothing more for me to say about it, yet he still could see I was holding back. He pushed me to tell him. Finally, I came clean.

"Jax, we've not said we are exclusive with each other. I know it's early, and I'm not expecting it, but I'm just not sure about going away with someone for a weekend when I don't know where I stand. For all I know you could be dating several other women."

He arched his eyebrows and paused for a moment. "Ahhh," he said. "Skye, do you want to be exclusive?"

I was thinking, *Hell yes, but what do I really say to him without scaring him away?* So, I tried to be as honest as I could while diverting the question. I said, "Well, I haven't seen anyone but you since I met you. I know it's early, and I don't want to push you or anyone into anything they don't want. I think it should be a mutual decision, and I'm open to discussing this more with you." I took a deep breath, shut up, and waited to see what would say back to me. I watched him thinking. He was calculating his answer.

He looked right at me and said, "Skye, I also haven't seen anyone but you since we met. I really couldn't stop thinking about you and only you. I was dating a few women before we met, but I stopped that the night of the party. I have a strong connection to you and need to see this through, whatever that entails. I would be devastated even thinking about you being with someone else. If you are inclined, I think we should be exclusive and see where this adventure takes us."

Without realizing it, I had held my breath the entire time. When he said those words, I started to breathe again. I looked directly at him and said, "Yes, I agree." And out of the blue, I got very emotional. Tears came, and he saw them. He took one look at me and grabbed me, hugging me close to him, as I laid my head down on his chest. Tears rolled down my face. *I am wanted.*

All In

He didn't ask but stayed the night anyway. He came prepared with his own bag and clothes for the morning. We spent the rest of the evening cuddling, kissing, and wrapped up in each other while watching television before going to bed. I loved this sweet time. I could relax, be vulnerable, and be myself without any thoughts of what was next or the anticipation of a move. I loved being affectionate but could not stand it when my affection meant just sex to a man. I wanted to be able to be touched, hugged, kissed, cuddled, and shown physical affection without it always leading to sex. When it did, I pulled the affection away, and that wasn't healthy or authentic for me.

Before going to sleep, as I wrapped myself into him, Jax said, "Mexico, yes?"

I said, "Yes."

A happy smile crossed his face, and I was rewarded with a wonderful kiss. He then said, "I'll take care of everything. You just show up. I'll let you know more tomorrow." And we both went to sleep happy. Initiator.

Early morning arrived, and again my brain and body wanted him. Again, I initiated. I loved mornings with him. We awoke from deep slumber, coming out of the beta brainwaves that had us traveling into the universe while we slept here on Earth. There was a softness to the morning for me. A vulnerability. A soulful connection. A deep sense of love. I cherished this time, even when limited, with him. It gratified me on so many levels.

After we were both satisfied, he got ready for work. He brought me coffee in bed, which I loved and would never get tired of. Acts of service is one of my prominent love languages. Quality time is my main one. This time, he took the liberty to shower and get dressed before he left. I found it interesting that he just made himself more and more at home. After he took off for the day, I went into the bathroom and noticed he left his toothbrush there. I pulled open a drawer in the bathroom and saw he had a few personal items inside the drawer. I'd heard of women doing this at men's places, but we were at my place because of Pepper. I was surprised to see this. A smile crossed my face.

I had to call my ex that day. I told him I needed to go out of town this weekend and asked if he could watch Pepper for me. I told him very little of my personal life. All I said to others about my former husband was that he treated me better as his ex-wife than his wife. We were friendly, communicated well about the kids and dog, and were both grateful our divorce wasn't horrific. Because we both were products of divorced parents, and those separations were acrimonious, we were committed to be our best selves for the sakes of our kids. I was proud of our handling of the split. My life was way easier because of this, unlike the countless new people I'd met who were still stuck, hurting, and trying to recover from their bad divorces. He could watch Pepper.

Jax called me that afternoon and got my personal information for the flight and booked me. He left Tuesday night because he had appointments, and he booked me to arrive Thursday night instead of Friday. I just went with it. He said he had a driver picking me up at my house to take me to the Atlanta airport. He told me which clothes to pack and explained that a limo would pick me up at the Puerto Vallarta airport and take me to the hotel. He had a late dinner planned with me (instead of with his co-workers) on Thursday. He did have to work Friday but would finish after lunchtime. He warned me to be ready for some fun. I was thrilled. All I had to do was pack, which can be a feat for us women.

The week flew by. He called me from Mexico when he landed and still reached out daily. I was picked up on time for the airport and was surprised to see he put me in first class for the flight. Sweet. It was apparent he did well, financially. He dressed the part, drove the part, ate the part, lived the part, and treated me wonderfully. However, I really didn't know much about what he did for work. A man's career has never been a real focus for me. Normally, it is all-consuming for them, along with golf and/or all sports, so I tend to just listen when they start talking about work. I am more concerned about their character, personality, and how I feel with them. However, I will say I've been fortunate to share time in my life with men that do well financially and have great careers, so I have never lacked financial security.

The flight was perfect. The limo driver was there on time, and he helped me with my baggage. We drove about forty-five minutes to the hotel. I was excited but tired because of the time difference. At the hotel, I immediately asked for some coffee. I didn't need to be falling asleep at dinner when Jax had done all this for me. With caffeine in hand, I checked in and followed the bellhop to the room. I was reawakened with the fresh, ocean breeze. It was already dark when I arrived, but I could feel the ocean. Relaxed renewal held me. To the top of the elevator shaft we went and all the way into an amazing penthouse suite. All-glass windows from top to bottom filled the entire two-story room. I could not wait to see the morning view of the ocean. Some of the doors were open, so the ocean breeze came into the rooms. The bellhop placed my items in the bedroom while I waited in the main room. I tipped him generously as he shut the door.

Jax wasn't there, and I was alone. I laughed with excitement as a sense of thrill overcame me. I walked throughout this amazing place he had picked. I looked at all the decor and details and then went into the bedroom. It was gorgeous and romantic. A bouquet of flowers lay on the king-sized bed. I read a note from Jax that said he had been counting the days. I opened the walk-in, custom closet to see half of it taken with Jax's items and the other half open for me. I unpacked, taking my time. Just when I finished, I heard someone. It was Jax. Literally, I ran to him and jumped on him, kissing him happily like a little girl. He swung me around, reciprocating my affection and smiling broadly. He said he was so happy to see me. What a dream! The caffeine had hit me, for I couldn't stop talking. I told him about the day, travels, location, what I was excited about, and all the nonsense talk we women love to share. He nodded in approval. I hadn't even given him the time to catch me up on his days, but we got to that. When I looked at him, it was the happiest I'd ever seen him. In that moment, I knew that this was exactly where I wanted to be and with no one else in the world.

After my excitement calmed down, we had dinner. Suddenly, I was famished. I needed to shower and get ready after the long travel day. Jax pulled out some healthy snacks for me from the fridge so I could nibble as I got ready. Of course he did. I asked him to pull something out of the closet for me to wear because I had no idea which outfit to grab. I had brought several options for everything I could think we might do. I packed super casual to very elegant to everything in between. I jumped in the shower and when I stepped out, Jax was in front of me holding the towel. I smiled shyly. He was so quick, quiet, and stealth. We both knew it was not the time, but he still enjoyed drying me off while kissing me sweetly all over. He knew not to give too much right then or dinner would be skipped. I took my time getting ready, doing all my normal beauty stuff, as Jax readied himself and watched me carefully. I talked most of the time. He mostly observed. I wondered, *A penny for your thoughts.*

He picked a sexy, silky, little black dress for me to wear. Once dressed, off to dinner we went. It was a sweet, romantic place with outside seating and lights hanging off the low trees. Soft music filled the air and candles lit the tables. We took our time. We flirted endlessly. He was softening me up like butter. I thought, *I'm the luckiest woman on earth,* for that was how he made me feel. I was falling hard for him. Thoughtful.

After dinner, we headed back to the hotel, and he asked if I minded if we swung by the bar to meet some of his co-workers. I didn't mind. I was flattered that he wanted me to meet them and that he wanted to bring me into his world. Graciously, they welcomed me like one of the team, cheering Jax on like he had won the lottery. They were as charming as could be. We laughed and had fun with this group of mostly men. Jax got to see me in a social business situation, which is where I shine. Years socializing in corporate America set me up with solid conversation skills. A woman needs to be able to handle herself independently at business functions. Her man shouldn't have to worry about how she handles herself nor feel like he must be attached to her hip. I was and am independent. After about an hour or so, we wrapped up. He held my hand as we headed off our own way. He complimented how I carried myself and said that the group loved me. He was happy, which made me happy.

My mind was on other things … pertaining to us. As we walked into the elevator, he read my mind as he immediately came to me, gently pushing me up against the mirrors, staring at me with that smirk before he began to enthusiastically kiss my neck. I fully accepted. Whatever he gave, I'd accept without hesitation or question. I was all in. I just prayed that he was, too. We hit our floor and I was already weak in the knees, grasping his hand as I stumbled out of the elevator. He held me close as we walked into our place for the weekend.

Thoughtful

I thought this was it, the moment. I was so excited and nervous, not sure which one emotion dominated. But my cool Jax wasn't like that at all. He adjusted to my moods. He made sure I was relaxed, comfortable, and trusted him. Holding my hand, he walked me into the bedroom, which had flowers all over the place, candles lit, music playing, and silk sheets ready. Is there a woman alive who doesn't love romance? I was touched and told him so by my expression. He gave me a moment to reflect and offered a quick sweet kiss on the cheek as he let go of my hand. Then I heard the bathtub being filled. I stood in awe, almost to tears, paralyzed by what to do. Jax was back.

He played "Invite Me In" by Wild Ones and took me in his arms where I felt safe. He started to sway, moving me with him. We danced, soft and close, as he held me. I looked up into his eyes, the clarity of them, the sweet soul, the well that runs deep, and I kissed him gently, taking in his full lips. My nervousness was replaced with tenderness. He would take care of me that night. Slowly, we danced into the enormous bathroom where he gently turned me in front of one of the many mirrors and began to undress me. Taking his time, he kissed me as he removed each piece of clothing while swaying, holding me, and I watched. All I could think of was his amazing ability to seduce me. A desire filled me that I had never known before.

Once undressed, he swayed me to the bathtub, and as I got in, he quickly undressed. Joining me, he sat behind me as I lay back against him. He wrapped his hands around me, pulling the bubbles up with me. Then he whispered. Oh, he knew me. He knew that to truly have me was to have my mind also. The emotional, physical, and mental stimulation must all bond as one. He knew, which absolutely astounded me. He whispered. He said only one word at a time. Without uttering sentences, he shared what he liked about me: the physical parts of my body, the way I felt, the depth of my soul, my laughter, my emotions, the way I thought. As he said this, he massaged my shoulders, my neck, and my back. Relaxing me, he whispered sweet love notes. He moved down the front of my body, touching my breasts and down to my blooming flower. He began to massage my nub as I relaxed more into his body. I felt his package from behind. He was gentle, very slow, taking all the time in the world. I felt completely connected to him. I started to turn toward him and face him. He pulled me up to kiss me. Then he looked right into my eyes and whispered, "I'm falling for you." That sealed the deal for me.

We got out of the tub, sharing a towel and quickly drying the super wet spots on each other before going to the bed. I sat down on the soft silk sheets as he began a sensual music playlist. I watched his every move like a hungry tigress.

He knelt down in front of me, and I reached to grab his face, sweetly kissing him. "Lovers" by Anna of the North began to play. He came up to join me on the bed. Lying sideways on the bed, we began together, both giving equally. Sweet kisses became more intense, we wrapped our bodies together, legs entwined, arms around each other, pulling closer, moving constantly. Rolling from sideways to me on my back, he moved his kissing, sucking, and licking down my neck to my breasts, then down my stomach, and then down to my pussy. He started licking everywhere, getting me super wet on the outside while my juices on the inside were boiling. He moved to my inner thighs for some sucking before climbing back up my body, sucking all the way back up to my face. Sarah McLachlan's "Sweet Surrender" played as we grew obsessively in our movements.

My turn. I flipped him on his back, sucking his face, moving down to his chest, to his stomach, and to his cock. I took his piece full in with my mouth, slowly sucking, soaking him up with wetness. He grabbed my hair and pulled me back up while he met me halfway sitting. I moved to sit on top of him without penetration, moving back and forth oh so slowly, kissing deeply, holding on to each other like it was the last time we would be together. My body was on fire, chills bubbled on my arms, and electricity flowed between us. Then I let him take the lead. He moved me to my back. He gave and gave. My senses overflowed. I smelled us and our sex emitting from our bodies. I heard sensuality in the music and our moans. I tasted all of him in my mouth. I felt his touches deep within my soul. I watched him, eyes wide open, the entire time. So in sync, our bodies never stopped moving. He talked, asking me if I liked this touch, this kiss, did it turn me on. He got one yes after another from me as I asked for more, telling him what I love and what works.

He paused. "Cola" from Lana Del Ray played. He said, "Repeat song." He stared at me with that hazy cloud in his eyes that I'd seen once before when he tried to overtake me. Tonight, I wouldn't resist. I'd let him lead. I would surrender completely to him. Staring at me, he said, "Don't take your eyes off mine," as he went down on me.

I watched him, meeting his eyes as he licked and sucked me, my body squirming with pure enjoyment, He teased, making sure I was not going to come now, as he watched me the entire time. He moved up, never leaving my eyes, and pulled me down low to him. My legs went around him to the outside. He planked over me, lowering to kiss me deeply, hovering his body over mine, telling me again to not let go of his eyes. Then he moved to kiss me down my body and onto his knees, he spread my legs wider, placing a hand behind the small of my back, he pushed a pillow underneath me while moving me up to him.

84

He slowly entered me. I gasped. My resolve dissolved. He was perfect inside me and a feeling of contentment overtook me. As he slowly entered me, he didn't move until he was all the way inside me. Then, gently, he began to move. And I moved with him, back and forth. Lowering me down on top of the pillow, he started to lean his body onto mine, and all of his pelvis was on me. His body rubbed my happy button, grinding into it, and we began to move in circles.

Our movements started to pick up in speed. I wanted to close my eyes but every time I did, he brought me back to him. I reached to grab him closer to me. I wanted more of him. He lowered completely on top of me, Kamasutra missionary-style. We never stopped. We kissed as I became more and more greedy. Wrapping his hands around my back, his intensity and my longing overtook us. Down the water well I went. This was Tantric sex.

Still holding each other, we rolled to the side. Then I was on top, and he was deeper inside me. He pushed my hips down into him, a little harder. I leaned down on him as he controlled the speed and movement. Grabbing my butt, pushing me down, he hit my g-spot, pumping slow but hard. Grasping, moaning, breathing faster, I was getting close. He grabbed my back. Making sure we didn't stop, he moved to a sitting position. We went into the OM position. For me, this is the most intimate position. I wrapped my legs behind him as he supported me in a total embrace. Our bodies could not have been any closer, and our faces met with passionate kissing, open eyes, connecting minds and souls as our bodies did what was natural. We both slowed down. We relished in the present moment, feeling everything that was between us. My emotions ran high with my body, and I started to tear up. He checked in with me, asking if I was okay, which I was. I told him I was just emotional, and he kissed my eyes as we began moving in perfect harmony. Deeper, harder, faster. As sweat started to slide down my back, he held me tight. The sounds from both of us were so sweet to the ears. I told him I was close as I unleashed all power to him. He took me completely, as my body rose back, I hit an intensely amazing orgasm. I closed my eyes. He grabbed my throat firmly, cutting some oxygen off, making the height of my orgasm even higher, but he then gently brought my face to him, demanding I open my eyes as my body climaxed again, this time with him. I waited until we both started to come down, but it was so physically intense for me that I wanted him out. I pulled off, falling down by his side.

My entire body was shaking like I had low blood sugar. Physically and emotionally, I was spent. I think he was surprised when I removed myself so quickly, and he went into "aftercare" mode. He rolled sideways next to me, gently touching me, asking me how I was, talking to me. I barely heard him. I was deep in my mind. I opened my eyes and told him, "I'm amazing and need sleep." As I lay there depleted, he moved me into spoon position, pulled the covers over us, turned the music off, and we slept.

Awake

When I awoke the next morning, I was shocked to see it was 9:00 AM. I never sleep that long or hard. The sun shined beautifully into the room. Jax had opened the curtains and glass door so fresh ocean air could come in. I relished in the sounds of the waves. He was not there. I knew he had to work until around lunchtime. I took my time getting out of bed. I went into the bathroom. When I came out, I grabbed his T-shirt from the floor, picked up his scent that I loved so much, and threw it on. I walked out into the main area where Jax had left me a note and brewed coffee for me. Thank goodness he knew I had to have my coffee in the morning. I picked up the coffee cup and the note and went outside on the balcony to sit. He had written, "Skye, as I watch you sleep this morning, my heart aches to leave you alone right now. I wanted to be with you at this moment. Last night was beyond what I could have ever expected. I cannot stop thinking about you. I will see you soon. Dress casually for lunch. Yours, Jax." I smiled softly with a warmed heart.

I decided to take a walk on the beach. As I pondered, picking up seashells, feeling the water, loving the breeze on my face, I realized that I was happy about getting my cobwebs out. It'd been a very long time since I had "done the deed." I had wondered if I'd even remember how. There'd been opportunities. There always are for any woman alive. If you're willing to give it; it will be taken. There's no question about that. But I had waited. I needed my first time (again) to feel like something special and with someone special. I had wanted it so badly all that time, was so tempted, but I waited. I still took a risk with Jax, not really knowing fully where he stood and that he could be a trickster, but I was rewarded. Today, I felt truly valued and cared for by Jax.

Once back in the room, I showered and got ready for lunch. I pulled out a cute sundress and low heels. Soon, I heard the door open. I walked out into the main area as I saw him coming my way. He quickened his steps, grabbing me around my waist, squeezing until I couldn't breathe, and plunged a wonderful kiss into my mouth. I would never have to guess how he felt about me. He'd show me all the time. Action was key.

He started questioning me non-stop. He wanted to know how I was doing, what I had done all morning, what time I woke up, if I got the note and coffee, if he'd made the coffee correctly, on and on and on. Finally, he asked what he really wanted to know. "How do you feel about last night?"

I answered all of his questions but the last one. That one, I asked the same right back at him. "Well, Jax, how do you feel about last night?"

He looked down at his feet. I'd not seen him hesitate before. I got panicky. So, I decided to answer first and let him off the hook. Feeling extremely exposed, I gave a quick answer, "I had an amazing night and couldn't be happier or more satisfied."

Then, I asked him again how he felt about last night. He looked up with a huge smile, but it was his eyes I saw. There was a softness to them, a vulnerability he hadn't shown. It melted my heart. While the entire time I was thinking about myself, all he was thinking about was me. This was important to him. *I* was important to him. My heart grew with love. I walked up to him, looked into his sweet eyes, and kissed him with all the love I had in my heart, holding him close to me. It was a tender moment between us, a memory that touched me and I will never forget.

Adventure

Jax changed into shorts and a T-shirt, and off to lunch we went. He told me that since it was our first day, he thought we could hang on the beach and then go jet-skiing. He ran through the rest of the weekend, asking my preferences on activities. I loved this. We decided together, but he made all the plans. I sat back to relax and enjoy. I love adventure, so I'm completely down to do most things. However, I also enjoy chilling out. Jax included me a little in each of our plans, so I was content. I knew I should embrace the present because the time would fly.

Casually, we walked down to the beach where an umbrella, chairs, small table, and towels were set up for us. I smiled because I like being taken care of. Jax tipped the guys. I also like manners. I watch how men tip. I cannot stand a cheap man. I don't have a problem with being frugal, living within means, and being financially smart. In fact, I believe these traits are important. I have a problem with being cheap. If a man is cheap, trying to scam someone out of his or her money, then he will be cheap with you. It is a character issue. Jax was generous with tips, as was I, and I appreciated his generosity.

We settled into our space. I wore a black halter bikini top with a skirted bottom. I usually try to hide my flaws. In my case, this baby's got back and bigger thighs, so I look better in a mini-skirt swimsuit than a bikini bottom. I have large breasts, so I try to focus the good attention there. After losing weight that past year, my stomach was flat but by no means tight. Like most women my age who are moms, I have that little pooch at the bottom of my belly, which is the most annoying issue. I dress and look age appropriate. Jax looked hot in his suit. I'd die to have his skin color and that base tan. I am always as white as a ghost. Women looked at him. He was slim and toned but without a six pack. I'd be intimidated if his body were significantly better than mine. He didn't seem bothered at all by my physical flaws and appeared to enjoy each part of my body equally. This was a huge relief.

Of course, I asked him to lather me up. I wanted to feel his touch. And he made it so sensual by easing through one area of my body at a time, rubbing in all the lotion, massaging me as he did it. My lust flared up. His turn. After applying lotion, we lay out as I soaked in the sun, just chilling, not talking.

Once we were both hot enough from the sun, he said, "Let's jump in the ocean." I followed him into the water. He dove headfirst. I was like a cat. I needed time to adjust to the water. I moved at a snail's pace and slowly waded in. He came out of the water right in front of me, grabbed my hand, and pulled me a tad deeper. He turned around to tell me to jump on his back. I did. He went right under as I tried to stay above. He came up laughing. Teasing, he said, "Go under, or I'll make you."

So, I plunged under, adjusting to the slight chill. I like bath water temperature. This was a bit cooler. When I came up, he was right in front of me and grinning wide. Then he planted a big kiss on my lips. He put his hands around my waist to pull me deeper into the water with him. There were not a lot of people in the water at that time. It felt like we had the entire ocean to ourselves. We played for a bit, laughing and having fun.

He went under and came up between my legs. I wasn't expecting that. He started to rub my muffin. I jolted alive. I looked around to see where the people were, how dark the water was, and whether anyone could see us. I thought we were far enough out. He came out of the water and grabbed me around the waist to pull me into him, so I wrapped my legs around him. I told Jax he was naughty. He liked it. He felt me out under the water, getting my juices flowing. Turning around in circles, me holding on to him, grinning like the Cheshire cat, I could sense where this was heading. He took me underwater with him, kissing below, then up again, laughing.

Back and forth we went. One time when we were under, he pulled my suit bottom off and handed it to me to hold. Up again. Naughty boy. Down again, he pulled his suit off and handed it to me. Up again. He was holding me. I was holding our suits. He plunged his head into my breasts with my top on and started blowing bubbles. I laughed. He smiled. Then he pulled me closer, adjusted, and put himself inside me. I gasped. We turned in circles, kissing, as he was pumping away so it didn't look like we were having full-on sex in the middle of the ocean near a public beach. But that is exactly what we were doing.

After the deed was done, the suits went back on. We still played around, releasing each other, floating around, and enjoying our own world before we headed out of the water. When I walked back onto the beach, I looked around to see if we were spotted by anyone. People glanced at us, but no one stared. I was relieved. We lay back down on the chairs. Jax ordered some drinks and a light snack while I tanned. Later in the day, we headed off to have some fun on jet skis. Playful.

Content

We'd had a full day in the sun and water, so when we got back to our room around 6:00 PM. I asked what time we needed to leave for dinner. I was hoping for a quick nap. He asked me if I was tired and I said yes, so he said he'd move the reservation to a later time. I went into the bed, set my alarm for an hour, and waited for Jax to confirm that dinner would be at 9:00 PM. He came over and sat on the bed next to me, moving my hair to the side so he could see my face. He kissed me sweetly as I lazily fell asleep. I slept deeply.

When my alarm woke me, I thought it was the next day. I dragged myself from bed, taking a moment to get my brain caught up to the correct time, and went looking for Jax. He was reading on the balcony. I walked outside wearing his T-shirt and a smile. He asked if I slept well. I stood at the balcony, leaning my arms on it, watching the sun start to drop. It was exquisite. I was a happy woman. I looked back at him as he stared me down. I forgot I had no underwear on, so he was getting quite a behind view from me. I laughed because I knew what he was thinking. He grinned. He stood to come to me, holding me from behind, and we watched the sunset together. He said, "Beautiful."

I replied, "Yes, it is."

He said, "I was talking about you."

We got ready for dinner. When I was showering, I saw him watching me and wondered when he'd join me. I despise being rushed, and he allowed me the time I needed. Ready before I was, Jax was on the phone when I came out dressed. He said I looked ravishing.

He picked another fantastic location with amazing fresh food. During dinner, I asked more about what he did for work, and he went to great lengths explaining his position to me and his career

92

so that I understood. I asked his perspectives on politics, religion, the state of the world, and a variety of other issues. I wanted to understand his points of view, even if we disagreed on some of them. I like to know where someone stands on certain matters.

I listened. To me, it is more important to understand than to disagree and argue. Most people won't change their minds, so what is the point in arguing? To no surprise, he was well-educated and intelligent with his stances. When he asked me the same questions, I spoke with neutrality in almost all of my responses. He took my responses in stride, but I was not sure he believed me. I am just not that invested in the ways of the world. I want to live life to the fullest, do the next right thing, learn, and grow into the highest vibration I can while being authentic to myself and others. Personal growth is my hot spot.

Back at the hotel, I was itching for some loving. Jax said, "There's a full moon. How about a walk on the beach?" So, I made a quick change to leggings and a sweatshirt, and we left for the sand. We held hands as we strolled down the beach in the dark near the water.

He started talking as we walked and did not look at me. He took a deep breath and said he wanted me to know that he was enjoying the time together and for him it had been perfect. He said he couldn't stop thinking about me and relived our intimate times over and over. He cared deeply for me, and his emotions were strong. He said that every time we talked and learned more about each other, he felt a deeper emotional connection. And then he stopped and looked at me, saying very clearly that he believed we were meant for each other and that he was falling in love with me. I was stunned, for I didn't think this last part would come this soon if ever.

My heart melted. I reached up to kiss him sweetly. He embraced me. I looked directly at him and said I felt exactly the same way.

There was such an intensity between us at times that we couldn't even make it back to the room. Going back near rocks and a small enclave, we attacked each other with heat. Ripping our clothes off, lying down on the sandy beach, we began turning each other on. My body was lit. Immediately, I was wet. Being out in nature and possibly being seen excited me faster. I took the lead and mounted him. He was rough with my body—grabbing, pulling, pushing. Nothing like last night. I bit him hard on his nipples. He bit me back. I moved fast, reaching my hands to hold onto the rocks above so I could push down harder. This wasn't going to last long for either of us. My sounds were animalistic. I didn't hold back. And when I climaxed, I screamed. He was seconds behind me, releasing his magic potion all inside. I continued moving until he told me to stop. I leaned down to kiss him, telling him I wanted more. All I heard in my head was Billy Idol's song, "Rebel Yell."

He said we needed to get dressed and out of there before someone came. I guess I really did scream. We quickly started walking back down the beach as some guards with flashlights asked us if we had seen or heard anything. We said no, and as soon as they were some distance away, we looked at each other with quick, secret smiles. Still holding hands, we started jogging back to the hotel. We hit the sidewalk leading to the hotel, and all Jax said was, "You surprise me."

Once in the room, we both jumped in the shower to get the sand that was plastered all over us off. He started laughing, and then I did. He cleaned me off and I did him. I wanted more, but he told me to settle down because he needed some time to recover. He laughed more and said he'd created a monster. I said I'd been deprived and had some making up to do. We continued laughing until we got out.

94

I threw on a sexy nightie, for I did want more and would tempt him as soon as I could. He threw on underwear and shook his head at me with a huge grin. "Come on, my little vixen; let's chill out for a bit." He sat down on the couch and reached for the TV remote. I sat on top of him, smiling from ear to ear. He leaned back and said, "Okay." Then we talked as he grabbed my ass closer to him.

So, I said, "What do you want to talk about?"

He said, "Let's talk about sex."

I'm intrigued. "Great! What about sex?"

The questions rolled off his tongue like he'd been waiting for this moment to happen. How often do you want it? When? Do your moods determine what kind of sex you want? What about just fucking? What turns you on the most? How can I make your climaxes higher? What are you not willing to do? What are you open to doing? How much can you take? What about sex toys? Bondage? Anal? Porn? Videotaping? Role-playing? Being overtaken? Rough playing?

I'm sure I missed something there. I answered each and every question he asked, some with serious thinking on my part. Others were easy peasy. The one thing that was a hard no was any form of group sex including threesomes. It was not my thing because I'd be jealous and probably couldn't emotionally get over it. Doing anything like that would be the end of us. I suspected he'd had plenty of this already. I hoped those desires were satisfied. I briefly thought that this man had sexual urges I didn't see coming and, at the same time, how incredibly exciting and new this would be for me. I needed more trust built between us, and he understood and was willing to patiently wait. In the meantime, I was more than willing to get in a great fuck since he'd likely had enough time to recover. I asked him if I answered everything to his satisfaction, which I did, and I went in for another round with my new favorite person in the whole wide world.

He woke me up early Saturday and explained we'd be gone all day. I gave him a look. I love morning sex and hadn't gotten any yet. He said, "No time, buttercup. Get up. We've got to get going."

Quickly, I got ready for a bathing suit and casual change of clothes kind of day. I grabbed a beach bag and put inside it everything I might need. He filled another bag. On the way, the driver stopped to pick up food and drink items. Then we headed to the dock. Jax rented a catamaran for the day for just the two of us and staff. *Hello, Mr. Wonderful.* He certainly knew how to treat a woman right. The staff introduced themselves to us and loaded up. Honestly, I felt like a queen. The sun was rising as we left the dock. It was chilly, and I hadn't packed a sweatshirt. Jax came up behind me, put his light jacket on me, and handed me coffee. I turned toward him to hug him and grab body heat. He held me close as we watched in silence the morning glow of the day.

The day was perfect. Dolphins swam with us as we moved out into the open ocean. I giggled with delight. I am a big animal lover, but dolphins are one of my favorites. When I let my guard down, I can become quite childlike while taking in experiences. I become curious, excited, and build lots of energy. I kept looking at Jax as I ran around the boat to follow the dolphins and talked non-stop about them. He looked amused as he calmly stood and watched me.

The boat went for a couple of hours, and we arrived late morning near an island. The sun was out, finally warming me to the bones. We stopped, and one of the staff members called us to put on wetsuits. I looked at Jax as if to ask, "What are we doing?" I love the water but was nervous. He read my mind and reassured me, telling me that we were going to swim to the island for a special treat under an arch. He promised not to leave my side while in the water and that the trip was perfectly safe. We got ready and jumped in. The cold water shocked my system.

We were handed some jet float packs that would zoom us there fast. The staff also attached a floater to Jax's system. I had no idea what was in it. We adjusted and he looked at me, asking if I was ready. I nodded. He grabbed my hand as we started up these new toys. We zoomed toward the arch.

After a minute, I let go of his hand because I felt comfortable, but he never left my side. As we approached the arch, we stopped the jet packs and used them as floats as we swam through. The water was crystal clear. We could see the bottom and so many types of colorful fish and coral. At the other side was a sight to behold. Paradise. There was a huge, white sand beach with a clear water hole in the middle. Not a person was in sight. We got out of the water in order to walk across the sand to the hole. This water wasn't attached to the ocean. Trees were scattered around with all types of birds and creatures in them. The site looked untouched by humans. As I peeled off the wetsuit, I walked around in wonder.

Jax set up whatever was in the float and laid our wetsuits out to dry. He called me over to him. I walked up to him and planted a nice, big, wet kiss on him, letting him know how beautiful this was and how much I appreciated it. This pleased him. He had set up a large beach towel to share our lunch. We sat down to eat and talk. I asked him how he found this place and if he had been here before. I wondered if he had done this for other women. The answer was no. Relief. Then I asked him if he was perfect, which made him uncomfortable. He said, "Hardly, but I want you to be happy with me." I said I couldn't be happier, and I'd always remember this trip and time with him. And I knew I would.

After some time, we finished up lunch. He wanted to go into the swim hole. He stood, pulled me up, then stripped down to nothing. I grinned. I followed suit. Fun. We were going skinny dipping. Why not? There was not a soul to be found. The water was warm like bath water. Finally, my type. We played—diving, splashing, laughing, grabbing—before we embraced. He swam while I rode on his back. He eventually turned me around to face him. We started kissing. Slow and sweet. His eyes were soft and vulnerable with love in them. He let out a moan and told me I drove him wild. We got out. Lying down on the towel, wet and naked, he began to fondle me. Kissing from head to toe, he gradually took me in and then went down on me. I looked up at the perfect sky, the perfect place, and could not believe this was my life. As he sucked and fingered me, I came nicely. After a few minutes, when my body came down from the high and the wetness was flowing outside of me, he entered me. I was delighted.

He waited until he was completely inside me before he moved and I with him. He flipped me over and lifted me to doggie style. Starting slowly, his movement quickly became a pump, deliberate and hard. There was no kissing, no coddling. He was in total control, grabbing hard on my hips, moving deeper into me. He reached forward, grabbed my hair, and pulled me up to him so that we were next to each other. He sucked the back of my neck, moved a hand forward to stimulate my already sensitive butter bean, and he pumped even deeper and harder. He whispered into my ear that he was close, which turned me on more, then he pushed my upper body down, face into the ground, going as deep as he could, hitting my g-spot. I felt another orgasm coming. Moving faster, oh so deep, he came with intensity. I could feel his body shake, his moans loud, and his climax stimulated my brain and body. I came again after him.

Carefully, I lay all the way down with Jax still inside me. He laid down on top of my back. I felt his entire weight, his entire body, and his entire being. After a few minutes, he slid down lower on me and slipped out while resting his head on my lower back and only half his body on mine.

Lying still, I turned back to look at him. His eyes were closed. He wrapped his hands around my stomach, and I lay all the way back down as he fell asleep on top of me. I didn't move. I wanted him to slumber against my skin. I couldn't sleep, but I treasured this intimacy between us and patiently waited until he woke up after a short while. All I did was think while he slept. I thought about my life. I thought about where I'd been, how I had gotten there, and how excited and lucky I was. I could not recall a happier time in my life with someone. I knew there were memories and previous times of joy, but in that moment, that time with Jax took the cake. I then believed wholeheartedly that all the pain and suffering in the past was worth every second just to be there that day.

He awakened and rolled off of me. My back ached with his weight. Not being a young chicken, I moved with caution. I certainly didn't want to throw out my back or pull a muscle. I scooted down to him and kissed him. I asked how he was doing. He laughed and said, "Amazing."

We'd been there for a few hours, so it was time to return to the catamaran. We cleaned up everything, ensuring not one piece of trash was left behind, and left paradise as we had found it for the next pair of lovers to enjoy. Jax helped me into the wetsuit and jet pack as we reentered the cold ocean and zipped back to the boat.

On the way back, I enjoyed the fun toy. We climbed aboard with the help of the crew and took off the wetsuits. I went to the back and lay down on the netting to absorb the sun. Soon, Jax joined me. He got close and wrapped his arms around me, but I teasingly told him to back off because he was blocking my rays. He laughed and lay back next to me, holding my hand as I soaked up the sunlight and all the love in the world while my soul and heart filled with glorious light. Content.

Trust

By the time we arrived back at the dock, I was crisp with a base tan in front and back. Jax was dark. I was jealous and told him so. He laughed. I loved his laughter, his smile, his smirks, his grins, and especially his naughtiness. I looked for ways to bring them out of him. The sun was just starting to go down, so the air cooled a bit. Jax put his jacket on me as we said our goodbyes to the staff, thanking them for a wonderful day. Jax generously tipped each of them, and we jumped into the car waiting for us. I leaned into him, resting my head on his chest as I grew tired. I fell asleep for a bit, and he woke me once we arrived back at our home base.

It was our last night there. Tomorrow, late afternoon, we would head back to reality. I put it out of my mind, for I wanted to live in the present. I walked into the bedroom, took off my clothes except my bra and underwear, and crashed into bed. I told him I needed another hour to rest. I didn't sleep but pulled a book out to read. He reclined next to me and just stared. I was trying to read and sweetly told him to stop staring, but he didn't. I closed my book and looked at him and said, "What is it?"

Smiling coyly, he said he loved me. He continued saying he loved everything about me. The way I looked, felt, smelled, tasted, my personality, my outlook on life, my emotions, my thought process, my communication style, my history and how I got here, my depth, my playfulness. All of it. Everything. He was sincere, speaking from his heart, and I believed every word.

I was speechless. He was so stealth and often surprised me. *Do I soak this in for what it is, or say it back to him?* I didn't want to overthink it. I needed a moment to process. I distracted him (so my brain could catch up) by kissing him hard with my eyes wide open and staring into his. He held me close, kissed me, and gazed into my eyes. I came up for air and said, "I love you, too." And down the deep well we went…

He canceled dinner out and ordered room service instead. We'd enjoyed a long, wonderful day. We were physically and emotionally spent. A familiarity and tenderness came over us as our movements, thoughts, and emotions started to mirror. I was relieved not to go out. I am a homebody at times and like to rest and restore, feeling completely comfortable in my space.

After dinner, I got up and told him I needed to shower. I played my music and was in the mod for Anna Wise's "Precious Possession." I stepped in. Jax was right behind me. I turned my face and gave him a soft smile. Jax started to wash my hair. So gentle. No one had done that for me before. It was sensual, and I loved the feeling of his hands slowly massaging my scalp, washing down my back, and rinsing me completely under the water. We both started to clean each other, soaping up, finishing down, and feeling tenderly over each other with the warmth of the water. I absorbed all the sensations. I gave him my vulnerability and submission. I lightly kissed him. We made sweet love standing up in that shower. A softness enveloped us as we consumed each other completely. In bed, I wrapped myself completely in him. I no longer wanted to have my own space. I wanted to be completely entangled with him and fill my body with his energy. He kissed me on the lips and then on the forehead and said, "Goodnight, my love," as I fell into a deep sleep. Adoring.

I woke up energized. I hadn't slept that well in years. Jax was still asleep. Finally, I had him where I could get my morning sex. I quietly ran to the bathroom then snuck back into bed. I turned some music on. I was taking him this morning. I went down on him, knowing exactly when he awakened. I actually enjoyed sucking, licking, and going deep down on his cock. It turned me on.

I started playing with myself as he began moaning. I was getting really turned on and moved to sucking, licking, and biting his body all over, coming up from the covers to kiss him intensely and bite his lips. He was alert and sensed I wanted a fuck. His eyes clouded over like before, so I knew he was going to throttle me somehow. He grabbed my entire face, pulling me up before he engulfed me with his mouth, sticking some of his fingers down my throat at the same time. Then he whipped me around onto my stomach. He grabbed a towel lying on the bed and tied my hands behind my back, tightly. He stood behind me. I really thought I was going to take the lead, but in a matter of moments, Jax was in full control. I took deep breaths. I told myself to release control and submit to him. He paused. He grabbed lube and slathered it all over my pussy. He came down to my ear and whispered, "Don't resist. I'm going to fuck you hard."

Without hesitation, as promised, he entered me hard. I gasped loudly. While pulling me up from my neck, choking me slightly as he dragged my body to hang halfway over the bed. He was releasing upon me whatever urges he had, and I had no idea what was coming. I couldn't even think. He pushed down on my back while thrusting at lightning speed. Then he pulled my legs into a Superman pose while he went even deeper, telling me to hold that position as tightly as I could. He was so hard and deep that my body was in shock. He went from standing to mounting me, pulling my insides up with him as he began to pump deeper and harder. He released my arms from the towel, but they were numb and didn't move. They fell to my sides. He was pumping so hard that my body was actually moving forward on the bed.

He grabbed the towel and pushed it under my head and neck. He grabbed my muffin as hard as he could and rubbed me. I was trying to find some enjoyment out of this, as I continually told myself to relax, submit, and trust him. He put both of his hands around the towel and pulled my neck up with a slight choke hold, cutting the oxygen off in spurts but not dangerously. Now, I really was not liking this. He released the towel and bent over to bite my ass hard over and over. I was going to have marks. I couldn't register what was coming out of my mouth (if anything) other than it was wide open. He took the towel and started hitting my ass with it, at first not too hard, but then he went to whipping it. He pushed me down with one hand as he pumped deep and whipped the towel against my ass with the other. He started to climax. He whipped me around onto my back, leaned forward, and came into my wide-open mouth. I spit it all out.

As he was coming down, I had no idea what to think. I wasn't even close to climaxing myself and tried hard to enjoy some of what had just happened. But overall, I didn't. He was rough. He took. He didn't ask. He didn't check in. He treated me like a porn star, which I was not. I was pissed. I got up before I unleashed my anger upon him. I stormed to the bathroom, locked the door, and started the shower. Once in the shower, I heard him try to get in. He repeated my name and asked me if everything was all right. I didn't answer him. I started crying and took a long, hot shower to release my pent-up emotions. How could he treat me that way? Everything was perfect. Where was the communication? Certain things should have been discussed up front. I was not used to that type of physicality and certainly hadn't been treated that way before. This was bullshit. He hurt me. This was not love.

He unlocked the door from outside while I was still crying hard in the shower. I couldn't look at him. He got in and tried to pull me to him, but I pulled back, telling him no. Obviously distraught, he sat on the bench in front of me. Immediately, he said he was sorry. I told him, "I don't care." I sobbed, asking him how he thought in any way that was okay without discussing it with me first? I told him, "That wasn't a fuck. That was just *taking*." I felt disgusted and used. He looked up at me with anxious eyes. He said he didn't mean to scare or hurt me. He agreed, saying that I was absolutely right that it should have been discussed and agreed upon up front. He should have checked in and didn't, and yes, he did take and not give at all, and for that he was deeply sorry. He reached his hand out for me to take. I hesitated for the very first time. He saw what was happening. It anguished him.

He stood and said, "Please, Skye," while he held me to him. Rigid at first, once I was up against him, I softened a bit. My sobs stopped but the tears kept coming. He turned the shower off and walked me back to bed. We lay down. He held me close. But I turned out of his arms and away from him. I said, "I trusted you."

Trust. It can take so long to build but only a moment to destroy. Most times, the trust isn't completely broken, but it can take an excruciating length of time to rebuild. All humans have broken trust. Nobody can claim innocence here. Jax would have to repair that trust if he ever wanted me back. After spending decades bringing my walls down, I had just put one back up.

Wow, this is how we are going to end the epic weekend, I lamented. We would be together all day until evening with travel. Jax brought me coffee and set it next to the bed, no doubt as a peace offering. I turned to the other side so as not to look at him. He sat down next to me. He gently started to rub my back. I tensed up. He looked to see the damage done on my behind. He lay next to me, holding me in a spoon and saying he was so sorry again. He told me that nothing like that will happen ever without mutual, up-front communication. He never wanted me to feel unsafe or feel bad with him.

I sat up. He wanted to talk. Fine. I'd go there. So I asked him, "Why? Why did you have the strong urge to do that to me? How many times have you done this? How many women?" I said, "I don't have a problem with bondage or rough sex, but you broke all the rules." Hello, communication is the first lesson in Bondage 101.

I told him he didn't get to manhandle me, ever, without permission. I can be tough when angered. I asked him if he'd been bullshitting me. I wanted to know if *this* was what he really wanted. If so, then I was out. I was not going to be treated this way. *Peg me as another notch to his headboard,* I thought.

He didn't like that comment at all. He grabbed his head and shook it. He was frustrated. I was not letting him off the hook. He didn't know what to do or say to me, and I was not sure there was anything he could do or say. But he tried. He begged for my forgiveness. He asked what he could do to make it up to me. He said he didn't want to lose me. I meant too much to him. He said that we couldn't deny the connection and love we felt. As soon as he said love, I was on his ass again.

"Love?" I said, "That wasn't love at all." Then I said, "See if you can get us on earlier flights. I'm ready to go home." This crushed him. I got up from bed, grabbed my peace offering, and started packing.

I avoided him at all costs. He walked in. I walked out. I said nothing. He kept talking. I put my EarPods in and listened to music so as not to hear him. It was rude and I know it. I played soft, tender music, and breathed with it, which calmed my body down. I felt the need to meditate, so I walked out to the balcony, sat down, closed my eyes, and began the process. I took deep, steady breaths of the ocean, feeling the breeze in my body. I went into my state of being, turning the world off, turning Jax off, and turning myself off so I could connect to the universal, abundant, loving energy that didn't disappoint.

After neutralizing my emotions and viewing them objectively, I released them. It was toxic for me to hold on. I asked for the unnecessary wall to come down. I affirmed that I could handle whatever came my way. Meditation had been my secret to moving quickly through all my previous pain. Releasing had raised my vibration levels high, attracting and not chasing all that is abundant in life. I refused to go backward in my progress. The intention was set to move forward. Always. I was not going to allow this hiccup to stop me.

When I came out of my state, Jax was sitting next to me in a chair. I took my EarPods out and looked at him. I tried to see him and meet him exactly where he was. He messed up, he was sorry for it, and the only question I had was if he would do it again? Did he learn from his mistakes or repeat them? I'd calmed way down. I could now look at him without anger. I asked myself, *What do I really see?* I didn't want to fool myself or walk away too soon.

He said he couldn't get an earlier flight because there was only one per day back to Atlanta. We still had a few hours here before going to the airport. I said okay. I looked up at the amazing sky and said, "I think I'm going to take a walk on the beach. Do you want to come with me?"

He was surprised, and I literally watched relief overtake his countenance. "Yes, of course," he said.

We strolled down the beach. I stopped often to look at seashells and such. He paused with me. After a while, I held my hand out to him and he immediately took it. I did care deeply for him, and overall our bond felt like love. I was not willing to walk away without making sure that it was the right thing for *me* to do. He was truly remorseful, so I decided to see if the lesson was learned. We held hands like old lovers and walked close to each other again. He stopped me and wrapped his arms around me as we stared out into the ocean. He nestled his head behind my neck and kissed it softly. He said he was sorry, he loved me, and thanked me for not leaving him. Finally, I turned to him. Looking into his eyes, I gently pulled his face to mine and kissed him earnestly.

Forgiveness

I forgave him. That was not the problem. I needed to see if I'd forget or hold the experience against him in the future. Resentment and punishment are not good traits, but we all make these mistakes in relationships. I think women are especially prone to "not forget." I would see if all my preparation for this relationship had truly grown me as a person, or if I'd revert back to some of my old ways. Remember, relationships are the truest test of personal growth.

We returned to the hotel to grab a bite to eat before going to the airport. Jax had us in first class. I pretended to sleep most of the way, resting my head on his shoulder. We landed nicely that evening. The driver was waiting and took our things. We had about a forty-five-minute drive to my house. Once there, I thanked the driver and Jax for a beautiful weekend. I wanted to end on a positive note. He grabbed my hand before I got out and said my name. I just left it at, "Let's talk tomorrow." I gave him a sweet kiss and walked into my home. Home sweet home. Safety net. Complete comfort. I unpacked and crashed into bed. My phone buzzed. I was about to shut it off. I took a quick look.

Jax texted me to say he was home, he missed me already, he'd had a weekend he'd cherish forever, and he loved me. He told me to sleep well, and he'd call me in the morning. I didn't respond and turned off the phone. I turned on trash TV and fell asleep watching it. I slept soundly. I spent an hour in meditation that next morning. I then hit Pilates class and ran by to get Pepper. I spent the day running errands and getting caught up. Jax texted me three times before mid-afternoon and left me a voicemail that morning. I ignored him. I just needed some time to make sure I was okay in the head. That meant time alone. I caught up on calls with a couple of close girlfriends, telling them all the amazing details of the weekend. I left out the last morning.

I wanted a relationship that was co-independent not codependent. I had been there and done that. In my marriage, I gave all of myself away, and that nearly destroyed me. I'd worked very hard internally not to repeat those mistakes. I knew what I wanted and what was healthy. I would accept nothing less. I chose me. Jax would accept it or not. His issues were his. When I did see him, a conversation was going to happen and some boundaries needed to go up, with sex rules. If he could agree and follow through, then we could continue moving forward.

I came home late in the afternoon to let Pepper out. I saw Jax's car in front of my house. Oh, boy. I had gone too long without communicating, and he was anxious. That wasn't my intention. I walked outside to the car. He got out with flowers in hand. I went to him, smiled, and gave him a sweet kiss.

I said, "I'm surprised to see you. Why aren't you at work?" We walked into my house. Pepper was going crazy and was apparently happy to see him. He said he left work early because his head wasn't in the game. He was worried because he had not heard from me all day. I apologized but offered no explanation. It was the first time he had walked past my threshold without kissing. I felt sad.

I put the flowers in a vase as he stood there watching me. We sat down. He pulled through his hair in frustration but started by saying he didn't want me to shut down or shut him off. He didn't know what to do and if we could talk about it, and I let him know what to do, he would. I agreed with him and explained we have to talk about sex rules so this will never happen again. I said we needed to set some boundaries.

Before, when we talked about sex, I was more general. At that moment, I got very specific. First things first, he must communicate what his urges were up front, what he wanted to do to me, and what he wanted from me. There needed to be a code word for both of us. Anything completely new for me needed to be talked about in a conversation during the day, not right before or during, so I had time to think about it and decide. If he was going to dominate, he must remain in self-control so that I never distrust him again. Multiple check-ins throughout are required.

As far as boundaries were concerned, he needed to understand that I like my personal space and time alone. I explained that I was not interested in day in, day out, constant companionship. I like communication and connection daily by texting and talking, though. I told him everything I enjoyed when we were in Mexico, so he knew. I stated that I love morning sex, but it needs to be lovemaking with intimacy and sensuality. All the other stuff, any other time, day or night, could happen—like fucking, bondage, his urges, etc. But in the morning, I need to feel loved. I saw in his eyes that he understood. We got through a few more items, including some of his, and came to an agreement. I was relieved, and so was he.

He reached over to me, and we started kissing. I paused and said, "Nothing's going to happen tonight. You need to rebuild trust." He nodded. We had a massive make out session and then played some music and slow danced for a long time. He asked to stay just for the night, and I agreed. We had a lot of soft tender moments the rest of the evening. He touched me here or there with kindness and love but nothing sexual happened. When we headed to bed, I wrapped myself into him. I felt an urge but shut that down in my head as he tenderly held me.

Undeniable

I woke up early. I stared at him as he slept. I wanted him, but I was unsure how to manage it because my emotions were all over the place. Softly, I whispered in his ear, "Jax." He woke up and looked at me. It must have been written on my face. He started kissing me warmly. I needed to get out of my head, so I told him I needed music. He played Prince's "The Beautiful Ones." Oh, how that was the perfect song, expressing all the emotions pouring from me as I fell under the spell of rhythm, desire, and love. I was vulnerable. I submitted completely to him, but this time he was loving, generous, and focused on me. Our lovemaking was a meeting of the minds, emotions, and souls as he assured I came first, then immediately he followed in such a beautiful way. Jax gave and gave. And, once again, I was all in. Forgiveness.

Over the course of several months, our relationship deepened. There was a rhythm to us. Usually, we got together once or twice during the week when he was in town and every weekend. He was romantic and treated me like a queen. He brought me flowers, took me out to nice dinners, shopping, theaters, movies, hiking, museums, music events, road trips, and the works. He didn't stop dating me. We talked a lot. We had fun. We were serious. We could go to the depths, something I always strive for in a relationship. We understood each other. We loved each other. We were connected. Sometimes, I thought, *How can I live without him?*

I cannot believe how easily we flowed. He could take all of me—my emotions, passion, sensitivity, soulfulness, crazy thoughts, and hurt, along with my playfulness, fun, and laughter. He didn't try to change me, nor did I try to change him. He accepted me for who I was and am. He expanded my thinking, I learned so much about myself in the healthiest of ways.

I was always excited to see him, we couldn't keep our hands off each other, and I was deeply in love with him. And the sex. When I thought about it, I didn't believe I'd ever had so much sex in my life. I got my sweet morning sex, fulfilling my soul every time. We had sex on lazy afternoons, we fucked at night, experimenting with sex toys, porn, role playing, dominance and submission, light bondage, and every position imaginable. We could go for hours. All of it was discussed up front so there were no surprises for me, and all of it was amazing. This allowed me to submit to his urges (which could be intense) and embrace them, while my level of satisfaction was through the roof. He turned me on in a minute. My body was used to him now and wanted what was coming my way. I climaxed super-fast, going from an average timeframe to about five minutes and with multiple orgasms. He was diverse. He adjusted. He could be turned on with the mundane as much as the "out there." He made sure I was satisfied every single time.

Paris

Nine months in, he said he needed to go to Paris for work. This time, he asked me to go with him for the entire week. I jumped at the opportunity. Paris. I had never been. Doesn't every woman want to go to Paris at least once in her life? The romance, the sights, and the shopping are fantastic. Jax told me to pack only one bag of super casual clothes, like workout clothes and lounge wear, because we'd go going shopping when we got there. Per usual, a driver picked me up and then we swung over to Jax's. We flew first class and landed when Paris was dark. The view coming in on the plane was sparkly. I was excited. A driver took care of our things, and we headed to a luxury hotel in the penthouse suite. Overall, I am pretty low maintenance day to day, but when I travel, I love first class all the way. Jax knew that about me.

The suite was beautiful. We were in the heart of the city. A balcony looked straight into the Eiffel tower. Jax said the next day he didn't have to work, and we were going shopping all day, so I should be prepared. He smirked. He'd been there more than a few times, so I followed his lead. We ordered dinner in because it was late. I couldn't wait to fuck him in Paris. And so I did.

Jax woke me up by eating me out. He was incredible in this department. Out of the blue, my body was alive, and while he was massaging my thighs, rubbing my clit, and sweetly tasting my womanhood, my wetness appeared. My entire body was relaxed and anticipated the surrender I gave him, knowing that I was going to be so satisfied. What he could do with his tongue amazed me. It really is the most powerful muscle in the body. As I got close to exploding, he entered me hard. I gasped every single time.

Slowly, he rose from the covers. He planted a big kiss on my mouth and pulled me up to him. He started telling me how beautiful

I was, how incredibly sexy I was, and how he was going to tie me up and have him all to himself. From the side, he grabbed one of the long silk straps we brought with us (amongst other fun toys). He flipped me over, sitting up while he wrapped the strap around my throat from the front and bringing it down my back. I moved my arms behind him as he tied them up around my wrists.

Grabbing another one of the silk straps, he gently laid me face down as he took each of my legs and tightly bound them together. I love the silk ties that leave no marks. They allow my body to move freely in them while still being restrained, and they feel yummy to the skin. Silk feels incredible against your naked body. I heard Vera Blue's "Hold" play.

I was all tied up and submissive to Jax, but he checked in with me to make sure everything was comfortable. My code word confirmed, along with a body signal as a secondary precaution before he blindfolded me and placed a ball gag loosely in my mouth. With all the time on his side, Jax loved to take advantage. He began by putting pillows around me—under my face, my chest, and my stomach—to give me comfort and support where he wanted it. He started lubing my vagina and ass up, so very important, so I would not experience any pain. He put my hair in a ponytail. He began by kissing, licking, and sucking my body from head to toe, sucking my face, sticking his tongue in my gagged mouth, placing his finger inside my mouth while pulling on the side of my face. I started drooling. I thought about how being blindfolded was one of the greatest releases of the mind. I had no idea what was coming, and the mental thoughts escalated the entire experience. That was my last thought as I completely surrendered to his urges. He whispered filthy suggestions in my ear. He devoured my neck and spent time on my weakest spot, the top back of my neck. My body relaxed more.

Down my spine, he licked then sucked on the way back up. He placed his hands on my hips, pushed down, and held me while he took his time tasting the entire upper back side of my body. Down to my ass, he sucked, bit, kissed, and licked all of it as my anticipation amplified. As he was enjoying this, I felt a light tickling sensation all around my back. Feather tickler. I began squirming because of the tickling, and he commanded I stop moving. I couldn't help but move and he knew it. He was next to my ear again, whispering, "You must stop moving or I'll punish you." My wetness flowed out of me as I groaned in desire. I moved more on purpose.

The tickler was gone and replaced by the flogger. He placed it on my back for a minute, just laying it there on purpose so I felt it and knew what was coming next. He checked in with me during that time. I was green for go. The flogger ran down my back as I stopped moving and tensed up. For just a second, I didn't feel it before it plummeted onto my backside. I released a deep moan. He was warming me up. Methodically, he used this toy to receive the effects he wanted from me. Softly, then harder, he whipped my bum, back, and flanks as my body aroused to new heights. He talked dirty to me while doing it. Dominating words ensured I knew he was in control.

Then he pulled me up by both my arms and neck, using the silk bonds, choking me slightly as my body rose to him. On my knees, he told me to keep my head and neck down. Keeping me in submission, he said he was going to fuck me hard, that I deserved this, that he was in control, and that I was his to do with as he wanted. My body released more liquid. I went from relaxing to tensing up every few seconds with never-ending anticipation. He grabbed my tits from behind, pushing my body against his, I felt his hard erection. While holding me there, he moved his hands to put one arm underneath my breasts as I quickly felt vibration on my devil's doorbell. He had pulled out the clit vibrator. Oh, so yummy.

I was thrilled. Pulling my ponytail back so my head was up, he whispered to me, "My body, my woman, my precious possession."

I was so electrified I could not wait until he entered me, and I may have come at that very moment. But my Jax liked to take his time, teasing, making me wait, getting me close then saying, "No, not yet." He understood me completely. He knew I needed the mental stimulation as much as the physical. I get bored easily. He wouldn't bore me.

I was getting close, and he knew it. He stopped with the vibrator. He released the ball gag from my mouth. Spit was all over my face. He licked it from behind, spreading it all around. I caught my breath, and then he plunged his fingers down my throat. At the same time, he pulled me closer to him, spreading my legs as far as they could go in the ties, which wasn't much. He wanted it tight on the bottom. He added more lube, although I was soaking wet. He then entered me hard. I heard Nine Inch Nails sing "Closer." He moved to the rhythm hard, pumping, moving faster, then stopping so I didn't climax. It was so deliciously tight down there. He pushed me down hard on my face, pulled my ass up high, and added an anal vibrator against me. I was close. I told him so he knew.

He said not yet as he reentered me so delectably and went deep to my g-spot. Round and round, harder, deeper, my mind was on fire, my body couldn't hold back. I made deep animalistic sounds and I screamed out as an intense orgasm overtook my entire body. He didn't slow down for me, adding to the height of my climax, and I almost couldn't take it. He released his powerful energy liquid inside me with his own animalistic sounds. After his initial release, he took it out fast, flipped me over, and stuck his cock down my throat and demanded I suck. I did. All the way down until he was satisfied and removed himself.

As he was coming down from his heights, he took care of me by quickly releasing all the ties and the blindfold so I could completely relax. He lay down next to me, kissing me softly on the lips and told me, "Oh, how I love you so very much." And I loved him.

Whatever I Want

Good morning, Paris! After a brief nap so my body and mind could recover, I jumped up like a little girl, running to the balcony and yelling for Jax to join me. "Look at this, look at that, what's that, can we go there?" On and on I went. He let me be myself and leaned against the post as he smiled widely. All the while saying "Yes, yes, whatever your heart desires, my love."

We headed to Avenue Montaigne and Champs-Elysees to get in some high-end shopping. When we walked into the stores, Jax pulled out his credit card and said, "Whatever she wants." I asked him about everything. I pulled outfits, tried them on, modeled for him, and asked his opinions. I wanted to please him. He sat back, store after store, as the driver ran in to bring out piles of bags to load into the car. The last place we stopped before lunch was a sexy lingerie boutique. That time Jax was not sitting back but had me sit down while he meticulously chose every piece he wanted to see me in. We were set up in a private showing room while he had me put on each item and model for him. I instantly knew when he loved something because the smirk appeared.

This one number was his favorite, for he got really serious when I came out in it. He told me to come to him. As I did, he pulled me on top of him while he smelled me, then started rubbing me, telling me that I was going to wear it that night. He wanted to devour me. I told him, "Not now." He released me, paid, and we headed to lunch. We went to an outdoor cafe, of course, and enjoyed a long lunch filled with amazing food. After lunch, I pushed to see the Louvre. He was so patient. I knew he'd done all of this before when visiting, yet he was happy to accommodate my excitement.

We toured and ended up shopping at Hermes, Versace, and St. Laurent afterwards, where he also shopped for himself and got us additional luggage before heading back to the room. The driver brought all of our items in, Jax tipped him very well, and I crashed on the bed. It was already early evening for me, but in Paris that time of day is still early. It had been decades since I'd been treated like such a princess. A woman and helpers appeared in our room, and the next thing I knew, all of our items were taken away. I asked about this, and Jax explained that the ladies would prep and clean all the items. They would then hang them for us in the room's closets while we were at dinner so that all was organized and ready to go. Wow, I didn't even know this service existed. Nice touch. The day was such a sweet memory for me. Generous.

After everyone left the room, I pulled Jax into bed with me to rest. I thanked him a million times for the day and for what he did, as well as how he made me feel special. I kissed him over and over. That pleased him. Then I said, "How can I make it up to you?"

He smirked, "I can think of about one hundred different ways." Naughty boy. I laughed and we rested up for about an hour before getting ready for a late dinner and night out in Par-ee. We headed to Le Ciel de Paris for dinner. It is a cool, modern restaurant decorated in oranges and grays. The restaurant sits high over the city. The views are captivating. The food is impeccable. There would be no deprivation on this trip. The service was great, and we shared all of our food, trying out new items. After dinner, Jax wanted to head out to a nightclub. This wasn't something we did often, so it would be fun to go dancing and see the nightlife.

The driver dropped us off on the seedy side of Paris, and down we went into an alley that led to a door. Jax gave a code to get in. It was loud, dark, and smoky. I asked him how he knew of this place. He said he'd been there before. *Hmmm.* He held my hand the entire time and told me not to let go of him. We turned the corner and spotted a lit-up dance floor. Half the people were wearing close to nothing or costumes, and it appeared to be a sex place to me.

118

Then, all types of people started coming up and propositioning us to do a lot of dirty things with them. Oh, my dear Jax—he had a darker side, for sure. I understand why he had told me not to let go of him. I could be taken and so could he. We went straight to the dance floor where cages of women and men were hanging. I was in awe as I looked around because, although I'd heard of such places, I'd never been in one. He took me close, looked into my curious and naive eyes, and slow danced with me. While others were gyrating, jumping, and going crazy to the beat and music, and practically having sex right there, he ignored the noise and made the moment about us. When I was with him, I forgot about the rest of the world, its problems, and everyone else. I was all about him.

We slow danced at first, with him holding me close and feeling me out from top to bottom and kissing me all over. No one cared at all, no one was looking, and we were in our own world, together. We had fun with it all, dancing to the music and jumping with the crowd. All the while he held my hand and did not let go. Back and forth we danced, with sweat dripping down my body. We laughed, seduced, and played with each other. I loved it when we played. He never took his eyes off me while I was observing and embracing the vibe.

After some time and some water, we went back to slow dancing. He talked into my ear and told me all the things he loved about me. He started fervently kissing me, getting more intense. Then he grabbed my hand and we walked into the back where there were different "sex" rooms. While walking past, I saw women dancing for men, men dancing for men, women having oral sex with each other while men jacked off to them, threesomes, and even a room of group sex. I had never seen that before. All types of costumes, role playing, sex acts … I saw just about everything but animals, thankfully. That, I cannot tolerate.

We walked slowly. Jax allowed me time to look, observe, and take it in. He knew my mind was curious. I told him I needed to go to the bathroom, so he took me there but said he was staying right at the door and to hurry up because that might be a scene in and of itself. He was right. Women were making out. A couple of them were having some form of sex on the floor. I stepped over them. There were men having sex with women in the bath stalls, but I found one empty and didn't get close to sitting on that toilet.

I hurried up while Jax waited for me. When I walked out, there were three women basically on top of him. While my eyes grew wide, he completely ignored them and just stared at me with relief. He grabbed my hand, the women stayed at bay, and we continued to walk. As we turned another corner, there were stalls like old phone booths. Most of them were full, with all sorts of couples doing different forms of sex. Oral, anal, regular. This was quite an experience. Near the end, there was an empty one. Jax pulled me inside. I gave him a look that asked, *What the hell are you doing?*

His expression said, *I've got you. Trust me.*

The little phone booth looked like it had a ledge to sit on one side and a full-length mirror on the other side. He sat me up on the ledge. I said, "Jax."

He replied, "Shhh, no talking."

The music was loud and sexy. He started kissing me intensely. I saw the cloud appear in his eyes. He quickly started to pull down the top of my dress, he left my bra on but pulled it down from the front, so my breasts were exposed. He attacked them. I leaned back, taking it in. I understood what was going to happen. Pulling the dress lower, he took it off and put it beside me. He moved quickly down my stomach, inching my body toward him. He pulled my lacy underwear aside and went down on me. I lifted my legs over his shoulders as I succumbed to the pleasure. As I became more comfortable with the entire idea, I stared into the mirror across and watched him go to town on me. I grabbed his hair and pulled him closer in, wanting more. A couple walked by, taking a peek. I didn't care, and it heightened my sexuality. When he knew I was toasty, he took me off the ledge, moved me in front of the mirror to lean into, pulled his pants down, and entered me from behind. I was so turned on.

Slow at first, we quickly got into fuck mode. He was sucking my back and reached from behind to rub my slit. I was watching us. He was watching us. The intensity was out of this world. As we progressed, our fucking went harder and faster. I noticed a couple, at an appropriate distance, watching us. I was not surprised. I knew our sex was hot and guessed it was their warmup. It really turned me on knowing we were being watched. I told him I was close, he knew, and soon we came together, watching each other in the mirror that seemed to be our intimate friend.

He grabbed me and pulled me into him, kissing the back of my neck while we came down. The couple watching moved on and went into their own "phone booth." I smiled at Jax and said, "I hope that we helped them." He laughed. He pulled his pants up, helped me get dressed, and we walked out of that club owning the night. Neither one of us spoke on the way back to our place. I rolled down the window to feel the sweet Paris night air as I laid my head on his chest and placed my arms around him. I was the happiest girl in the world. Contentment.

The next morning, we woke late and Jax had to get to his work. He handed me a list of places to see or visit, suggested where I may want to eat for lunch, told me I had the driver all day, and checked to make sure I'd be okay alone. I am pretty independent and said, "Yes, of course. Don't think twice about me. Go do your work and bring home the bacon." He laughed, kissed me sweetly, and headed off to shower.

I started my day slowly because we'd been out late. I replayed the night before, and I realized how Jax pulled me out of my comfort zones. He was really good for me, giving me vitality and excitement. I knew I'd never be bored with him. I was madly in love. Jax understood me completely, loved me for who I am, flaws and all, handled my emotions, listened, and validated me. I shared everything with him. Our connection was real and deep. We didn't fight, we communicated well, and we discussed and debated in healthy ways. There was always a resolution or compromise that brought a win for both of us, and an end result we liked. I had never in my entire life felt so loved, and the bond was healing, healthy, and life-giving to me. Through our relationship, core trauma issues (that many women carry) healed. I looked to improve myself daily and aimed to please him immensely. I was strong, independent, and in charge of my life, but with Jax I could be vulnerable, soft, submissive, and a complex, feminine woman. His strong masculine energy balanced me and brought out the side of me that I'd always wanted and needed. I could not imagine my life without him. My heart was full.

When I thought about him, I felt incredibly blessed. He was good looking and had a great body for his age. Women stared at him all the time. He was in my age range. I found out when dating that I want men in my age range, but they want women ten years younger. I kept getting asked out by men who were "sugar daddies" (at least ten years older than I) or worse, married. I was truly disgusted when I was on a date and figured out the man was married. Marriage is sacred. I felt sorry for their wives.

I didn't sleep around, I didn't go crazy, and I had zero interest in one-nighters where the next day I would feel cheap, used, and left. It took me a while to learn to weed through the players, fuck-me-oncers, non-committers, party boys, mama's boys, puppy dogs, and liars. Jax was a true diamond in the rough.

What surprised me most when I reentered the dating world was how emasculated men were. They didn't initiate. They wanted the women to take charge, ask them out, hit on them, be the aggressor, and chase. I was shocked. They didn't chase, and I didn't chase, so we ended up in the friend zone. Many potential men became just friends for this reason alone. More shocking to me was how men I adored because of their calm and cool personalities were sitting back and getting laid all the time by different women. Many were one-nighters, but even the women who held out a bit of time still were left high and dry by these guys. These sleazy guys didn't have to do anything but buy a drink or a dinner. Now, I am all for female empowerment and am sure many of these women wanted to do the deed with no strings attached. To each their own; however, I still couldn't believe how many single adults don't want a relationship. Why? My guess is they don't create emotional connections. Physical attraction must be there for sure, but that lasts a minute, while emotional connection is how men fall in love (and sometimes faster than women). While I had no problem taking charge, I wanted a masculine, kind man. I wanted a man who chased me. Maybe it was old fashioned, or maybe I was tired of being in charge. Either way, Jax was well worth the wait. He chased and didn't let go. I got exactly what I asked for from the universe and was grateful daily.

Sometimes I wondered if Jax would leave me. Would I bore him? Would he find a younger, sexier version of me? If my well ran dry, would he go off to find more water? He had said, at times, he never planned to marry again. I wanted to marry again at some point. Would that be the end of us? Before I let my insecurities and anxious thoughts take hold, I released them because for today, he was here. He was present. He was mine. And I was thankful.

Pleasure

I spent the day leisurely taking in the sights, stopping at an outdoor cafe for lunch, casually walking, and listening in on French conversations, even though I didn't know what they were saying. I do like to people watch. Jax checked on me in the afternoon to make sure I was content entertaining myself. After a long, beautiful day of exploring, I decided to head back to the hotel to take a nap since I was still tired from staying up late last night. I slept like a baby.

I was awakened by my man sucking on my toes. Jax said, "You have beautiful, sexy feet." I've been told this many times in my life and dated someone who had a foot fetish. I remembered how incredibly surprised I was to see what someone with this desire could do with feet. He was in a sensual mood, so the pleasure would be mine. And it was.

That night, we went to another amazing restaurant. There were so many in Paris that it felt like it would take forever to taste the city. After dinner, Jax surprised me with a trip to a sex shop. There, we casually browsed, deciding sometimes together and sometimes not on the many toys to buy. It was like a normal store. People just walked in like nothing was unique about the place. I gathered that Europeans are freer with their sexuality. I asked Jax about several items I had never seen. He knew most of them. I thought to myself, *Sometimes it is good sense not to ask too much about someone's past unless he obviously wants to go there.* I believed it was better for our relationship if I didn't know too much detail of Jax's past sexual exploration. I just accepted it. After getting our fun stuff, we headed straight back to the hotel because, well, we had to try some of it out.

I could figure out Jax's moods by the music he played. He was a Scorpio, so the moods went right along with the excitement. Once we got back, 112's "Peaches and Cream" started playing, and he grabbed me and started to dance in the middle of the suite. We laughed, played, and turned it into a seductive dance. He felt my body, kissing and licking my neck in front then turning me around to kiss the back. Seducing me, he said wildly dirty things in my ear to get my body lit up like a Christmas tree. I was facing the outside view with the Eiffel tower in sight. Taking his sweet time, he started to undress me, unzipping my dress, kissing down my spine, letting the fabric hang on me. Pulling one side off the shoulder, he sucked from my collarbone down to my fingers and back up underneath my arm. He licked my armpit. Down the side of my flanks, he kissed, sucked, and licked harder. Up the other side, he repeated.

I was about to take my high heels off when he said, "No, keep them on." With only a sexy bra, thong, and heels on, I stood near the window. He danced me out to the balcony. Depeche Mode's "I Feel You" played. What a sensual, sexual song. There was a slight breeze, but it was not cold outside. He moved me to the railing while the breeze blew my hair back off my face. I was staring out into the twinkling lights of the Eiffel tower while noticing a man across the way standing by his full-size window and looking out. Briefly, I wondered if he saw us.

The lights were in full bloom in our suite while it was dark outside. I was sure if someone looked directly into the room, they would view quite a scene. Jax quickly pulled my thong to the side leaving it on along with my bra and heels. He warmed me up, rubbing my tender box and using one of the new vibrators to get me quickly ready. He put on a cock ring. He stood and folded me over the railing, with me holding on and leaning over it and my back half in his control. I anticipated and let out some moaning breaths. Strongly, he spread my legs wide as he entered me from behind. He felt so good to me. I could not have enough of him or his love.

Holding my hips tight, his fingers dug into me as he went into me with a teasing start and a hard forceful push right up to my g-spot. Yummy. I love a great fuck, and he was fucking me amazingly well, making me want more. Controlling my body to his pleasure while my mind was high, I glanced across the way. That man was still standing there. I knew he was watching. He had dropped his pants and was jacking off while holding one hand on his window. It turned me on to a new level of high. That man looked good from across the way. I could tell from the outline of his body. I almost came just thinking of him watching us. I definitely had caught the taste for voyeurism.

I let Jax know we were being watched. He knew it was turning me on more, so he said things like, "Do you want him to come over and do this to you? Do you want to suck his dick? Do you want to take us both on?" I couldn't take it as I imagined the scenes, and I hit my pinnacle orgasm. Jax followed suit. As we came down, Jax pulled me up from the railing and held me from behind. My body quivered from the release. He held me tight against him as we both stood. He wrapped his arms around me, whispering sweet notes in my ear and kissing my neck. I stared at the man across the way. He disappeared as Jax and I stood watching the lights twinkle on the tower.

The rest of our time together in Paris was similar. Jax didn't work the last two days of the trip, so we had full days together to enjoy more sights, long lunches, tender moments, handholding, kissing, intimate talks, and plenty of sex. I'd opened up my entire being to this man. There was a form of mind reading with him, and our intimacy was out of this world. We had complete trust, comfort, safety, and so much love.

My mind was stimulated when we had conversations. He was intelligent, and we had a high emotional connection. We talked all over the place on every topic out there. We could disagree on world, political, and spiritual issues but still be open to listening to each other with respect. He had changed my entire viewpoint on money and taught me how to relax with it and enjoy the comfort that it brings. He continued to be romantic, making me feel like a queen. He helped me in any way he could, often lifting burdens off my shoulders. We continued to live separately. He appreciated and respected my need for solace and independence. I knew he needed the same. He laughed that I loved my naps, but admitted it was his favorite time to watch me. My vulnerability, receptiveness, and acceptance of him kept him coming back. The fact that I met a man who helped me completely let down my guard amazed me.

Jax made me feel loved. More importantly, for the very first time in my life, I felt I deserved it. Now that I knew the feeling of being truly loved, I also knew I would never settle for anything less. I was living my best life. The morning we left Paris, I was allocated my sweet, sensual lovemaking. So many adventures on the trip were ingrained in my memory. My sexuality, confidence, and personal growth was expanding. I swore I looked thinner, younger, and had so much vitality—all because I was loved.

Anniversary

By the time we'd been together for two years, we'd made several trips inside and outside the US. I went with him on many business trips. We both loved to travel. We had a rhythm, comfort, and ease with each other. The sexual chemistry never ceased. In past relationships, by this time, reality had set in, and sex lessened because the initial high was gone. A "real relationship" took hold. However, with us, we still had both. We were together once or twice during the week and most weekends, and the sex was constant. Two or three times a day. I was never bored, always satisfied, and always wanting him.

I loved having my life away from him, doing my usual activities, keeping my relationships with family and friends going strong. He was not one to hold down, either. We accepted each other completely, not trying to change anything about the other. We did talk about flaws and annoying traits. We also called them out to each other but did so only to improve ourselves and never to shame the other. When we argued, which was rare, I could become very heated. He listened and validated me, so I did not escalate. That was soothing and healthy for me. I never held anger or resentment toward him. I chose to let go and move forward. He was calm and didn't anger easily. I grew. I learned. I loved. I accepted. I trusted. I healed.

Around this period, I felt the strong urge to form a stronger commitment with him. I wanted to marry him. I wanted to spend the rest of my life with him. I could not see myself with anyone else, ever. I wanted to grow old with him. I wanted sex with him. I wanted all of him, always.

I started dropping hints. I asked him more specific questions about his future, his dreams, and what he wanted. I was starting to push. I could see it in his eyes. I was on dangerous ground, for this was an area he avoided like the plague. He replied with compassion and kindness. He let me know how committed he was to me, how much he loved me, and how much he wanted to be with me. However, he repeatedly said, "I won't marry again. I really need for you to understand and accept this. I won't ever be tied down. I believe it's the death of a relationship." He was free, untamed, and wild.

I was free, domesticated, and trained. This was where our serious gap was. This was the weak link. This was where I had to truly decide if I could be a girlfriend the rest of my life, knowing that one day he could easily leave. He could leave me in a month, a year, ten years, twenty years, or never. In my mind, not getting married was the easy way to just someday walk away. I knew I didn't want that. I just didn't know if I could accept his hard stop. I strove to feel the safety of a marriage. I wanted to know that someone had my back, loved me unconditionally, and was there with a legal, financial, and moral commitment. I also knew myself.

Once I get something in my head, I am a force to reckon with. I had to decide if I could accept his choice and let go of him or take the risk and push my agenda. Plus, I was not getting any younger, and that big bad world of dating is not my cup of tea. I did not want to "go back out there" older and less physically attractive. A rush of previous insecurities surged through me. There was something there, inside me, that I needed to pay attention to and fix.

To celebrate our two years together, Jax asked me where I'd liked to go—"anywhere in the world" with him. I took a glance at my bucket travel list and said British Virgin Islands, preferably on a yacht. I smiled wide with that last request. He walked over to me, planted a deep kiss, and said "I'll take care of it."

I loved his initiation. I didn't have to do all the planning, scheduling, or work. He did most of those things, or maybe his assistant did. We agreed on the time based on his work schedule and when he could take off for a week. The trip would be around six months from then, when he had time and the weather was best. I left it all in his very capable hands. Gifts.

Time

Like a little girl, I was super excited about our trip. This was a dream come true. I'd wanted to go to the British Virgin Islands forever, but in the best way, which was on a boat, or in our case a yacht. About a month before our trip, I doubled up on my workouts and cut back on food to tighten up so I could wear bikinis all the time. My body was exactly where I loved it. Thin in the stomach and arms yet curvy in hips, butt, and thighs. I'd worked hard to get it there. I was certainly not the youngest or hottest woman I knew, but for my age I looked damn good.

My face is pretty. Being in love and smiling becomes you. I felt great; however, I wanted to *look* great to keep Jax's eyes on me instead of looking at all those younger, hotter women that he could easily get. He told me all the time he loved my body, and, more importantly to him, how my body felt. To this day, because men are visual beings, I believe you have to catch their eyes with a warm smile, eye contact, prettiness, and a body they like to look at. After that initial visual and a brief amount of time, it is more important for them to enjoy the connection and feel good. They become comfortable with your body, even though it's not perfect. Plus, Jax and I liked to watch ourselves in the mirror. I wanted to like what I saw.

Once we landed at the main island, we headed straight for the yacht. There was a crew of five, including the captain. It was just us. I was spoiled. The yacht could easily hold ten passengers, so this was indulgent for two people. I was wowed. Jax was smiling from ear to ear as he watched my mouth drop at this precious beauty. Not easily impressed with material things, he got me on this one and he knew it. We were introduced to the crew, and they showed us to the main suite.

It was stunning, large, and had the biggest round bed I had ever seen. Mirrors were everywhere. I jumped on Jax like a girl in a chocolate shop. He laughed at me. I kissed him all over, thanking him and pointing out all the nice things. I jumped on the bed and told him to join me. He smirked and said, "Hold on love, first things first, got to take care of business." He left me to unpack, unwind, and (of course) nap because we'd traveled all day.

I woke and headed out to the deck. We'd left port and were on the open ocean. A gentle breeze warmed my face. I walked out to the back of the yacht, spotted Jax on his phone, and quietly sat down next to him. He soon hung up. He came to me and climbed behind me in the lounge chair to hold me close to him as we watched the sun set in comfortable silence.

After a light dinner, I could not wait to get my hands on Jax. That bed with all the mirrors surrounding it was calling me. I asked, in private, one of the crew members to deliver to our room a basket of fresh mixed fruit, sugar, honey, and a change of fresh sheets. I winked and told them to skip the dessert after dinner. I wanted to play, so as soon as we hit the bedroom after dinner, I changed into some sexy lingerie. My requests were waiting in the room so we wouldn't be disturbed, as we had a long night ahead.

I started playing the INXS song "Need You Tonight" so Jax knew exactly where I was headed. I came out of the bathroom, and he was lying on the bed, wearing only his underwear with an enormous smile on his face. He knew what kind of mood I was in. I turned the music up loud because I had no idea where the crew was or what they could hear.

I started flirting with him by saying naughty and sexy things. He was so hot. I moved the fruit items closer to the bed and he asked what they were for, as if he didn't know. He asked what I was going to do with him since he was so vulnerable and exposed. What a tease. As I climbed on top of him to kiss him, he grabbed my ass and pulled me down. I sat up and said, "Oh no, you've been a very bad boy and must pay for it." Seductively, I moved to my suitcase and pulled out some tie up bonds. I grabbed a riding crop. I changed the music to Def Leppard's "Bite Me" as I forcefully tied his arms to the bed and left his legs free. I covered his eyes. I started by kissing him around his face and neck but soon bit down his shoulders, stomach, and legs. I flipped him over and bit his ass, hard. He moaned loudly. I remembered not to leave marks on his body because we would be exposed in bathing suits on the trip. So, his sweet butt would get the brunt of my attack.

As I continued to arouse him, I grabbed some of the fruit with the juices flowing. Flipping him over, I demanded that he open his mouth so I could feed him. First, I gave him a strawberry, making sure the juice flowed down his face. I licked the juices as I told him to eat. I asked him what it was, and he said strawberry. I rewarded him with a long deep suck on his cock. I checked in with him to confirm the code word and make sure he didn't choke because we were about to get heated. He was happy to comply. I grabbed an exotic fruit, one I was guessing he wouldn't know. "Bite it. What is it?"

He guessed wrong. I told him he must be punished. I flipped him over and cracked the riding crop hard on his ass. He gave a yelp followed by a moan. I asked if he was okay, and he said yes. He knew I was going to go hard on him if I was starting this way. I made sure he understood. I poured the honey all over the front of his chest, stomach, and dick. I asked him what it was. He guessed wrong. I licked some of it up, told him he was wrong again, and he tightened up as he knew what was coming. I was enjoying every ounce of this and got so turned on in the process. Flipped, I got him twice with the riding crop and then teased him with a bite. Flipped, next fruit. I gave him a banana. He got it right. I sat on his rock-hard cock and didn't move. I just sat on top of him. He started to move, I lightly slapped him and told him to stop, pushing his hips to a standstill. I took a moment for myself as I felt him completely and deeply inside me. The feeling was so natural, comfortable, a perfect fit.

Our physical relationship was wild and fun, but soulfully, I loved him. I pulled up fast and hard, leaving him with nothing. I licked more of the honey on his body from his waist all the way to his mouth. I grabbed the sugar and cunningly placed it on his nipples and dick, rubbing it in all areas. I poured a little honey on my hand, dipped it in the sugar, and placed my entire hand slowly into his mouth. I told him to lick and suck. This really turned me on. I asked him what it was. He got both right. I went down on him, beginning with massaging his inner thighs, licking and sucking all below his penis, up and down around his ass, scrotum, balls, and everywhere but his cock. He was starting to go crazy.

I spent some time there before the next test, allowing him a moment to relax and enjoy. Next fruit. Wrong. Flipped. Three times hard with the crop, three times hard with the bites. He was getting marks now. I checked in and got the green light. I left him on his stomach with his arms crisscrossed and twisted. I grabbed the juice from the fruit and slowly poured it on his back and ass as he twitched at each spot where it fell. I sucked all of it off his skin and all the way down to his ass. I sucked and lightly bit, licking every ounce of it up. I continued our game until all the fruits had been tested, with many successes and failures. I made sure he ended in success. As he waited for his reward, I grabbed a vibrator. I adjusted my lingerie, keeping it on but exposing my breasts and ass. Then I sat on top of him again, this time riding him hard, deep, and pulsating as only a tease would do. He called to me, asking for release, so I gave it to him.

He immediately grabbed me, ripped off his mask, and threw me around so we were in cowgirl style. He held me tight around my hips but let me continue the control and speed of the movements. I could feel he wanted to take over. His strong, masculine dominance always won. He'd allowed me to have my fun and he enjoyed it, but now he wanted to control. I submitted.

He pulled me off him as my favorite fuck song began to play, Katy Perry's "Dark Horse." There is nothing like the rhythm of that song to heighten my arousal. He flipped me to doggie style as he pulled down on my breasts hard and slid himself right inside me. He grabbed the crop and the vibrator. I told him I wanted to be fucked hard, so he knew exactly what I was shooting for. As he moved to the song, he hit me with the crop but not as hard as I had hit him, and I moaned loudly. I was going to enjoy every ounce of this.

He slid his lubricated thumb in just the top of my ass, pumping harder. After enjoyment with the crop, he threw it down and moved to the vibrator. He took it to my front and started moving it around my clit as he pulsated slower in me. I was in heaven. Sex did not get better than this. I wouldn't last long. Then he unleashed and I was rewarded. He went fast, deep, and hard, lying on top of my backside as he moved the vibrator from my cherry bomb inside me along with his cock so that I had the best of all worlds. I was losing all control. My sounds were animalistic and deep, and so were his. I yelled out his name, which told him I was close. He finished.

Oh, so strong. My orgasm was so high that not a peep came out of my mouth. My mouth was hanging open and wanting to scream as the intense height of complete euphoria consumed my entire physical body. I shook uncontrollably because all of my energy was in that climax. Jax came with me at the same time, making the satisfaction hit a new level in the astral plane. Collapsing upon each other and entwining our bodies, we fell fast asleep. Euphoria.

Commitment

Our time together on the trip was quality. We talked, laughed, and played. Almost always in bathing suits, we soaked up the rays until our bodies were sun-kissed tan. The crew told us they could not believe how beautiful we were together and how they wished to have this kind of love and compatibility. The weather was outstanding for the most part, with a fresh, ocean breezes daily. We went from island to island, exploring the sites, shopping, eating, and learning the history. We swam with dolphins in the wild and made love in the ocean and all over the yacht. You would have thought we were twenty years old and on our honeymoon. We were physically joined that our bodies were almost always touching somewhere. I loved to give him affection because he gave me love.

Mentally, we were so conjoined that words were often left unsaid. I had never felt this way with anyone, and it became all-consuming to me. He gave me strength and power; I was his weakness. Our emotional connection was off the charts. He knew everything about me and I him. There was no secrecy, distrust, or anger. We were on the same team, working together to be the best versions of ourselves and digging deep to heal the inner wounds created by others. I could not imagine ever being with anyone else.

Nearing the end of our weeklong journey, at dinner one evening, I told him that I wanted to be with him for the rest of my life. I erred on the vulnerable side, which opened him up to me so that his reactions wouldn't be harsh. I presented a speech to him that detailed why we should be together, how I felt about him, and exactly what I wanted. He listened with kind, sad eyes as I made my strong case for us. After my speech was over, which was long, he settled back in his chair and just stared at me. I must have looked pathetic, almost begging him to go to the next step with me. He tapped his finger, about to say something, then stopped himself. He looked at me. I watched his expression change from joyful to serious, and I knew that I was about to get a handful. Before he began, my heart sank, my hands became clammy, and I teared up.

Clearly and without doubts, he said to me, "Skye, we've talked about this several times, but recently you keep bringing it up. You know how I feel and why I feel this way. I love you so much, and I don't understand why you cannot just accept our relationship as it is. I agree with you on so many levels, but I'm never going to change my mind about marriage. I don't know what to say to make this any clearer. It makes me sad that you cannot stay present with me in the moment but need to project this unfounded belief that marriage is going to make us stay together. I feel marriage will be the beginning of the end for us."

He was the river that flowed forward, moving constantly, never stopping, everchanging. I was the pool of water at the bottom of the river, trying to collect its abundance, stopping its flow, wanting the wild water to stay within me.

He continued, "I need this to stop coming up, so let's once and for all talk this all the way through so we don't ever need to talk about it again." I was getting upset, and so was he. We left dinner and went back to the room. For hours, we hashed it out. It got ugly. I was an emotional fighter. I yelled, but he stayed calm. He was firm and took a mountain stance without budging. I was hysterically crying, with all of my deep wounds at the forefront of my space.

I felt an overwhelming sense of rejection. My mind couldn't understand why, if he loved me so much and everything was so easy with us, how he could not *want* to marry me. Why could he not make this commitment? I tried to understand where he was coming from, and to a point, I did, but ultimately it didn't make sense to me. I was fifty-three and didn't want to spend the rest of my life with someone who could quickly walk out whenever it pleased him.

I wanted someone who would fight to save the relationship when the tough times came. I was a committer.

This was who I was, and I wouldn't change it for someone else. I had done that for decades already. I'd learned my lessons and refused to repeat old mistakes to accommodate. He had his wounds, too, and they were right in my face. We could not come to an agreement. Extremely frustrated, hurt, and tired, he made his final warning to me. "Skye, I won't change my mind. Either you accept this and drop it from this point forward or make a decision that is best for you. I hope you choose to stay, because I love you so much, but you have to do you." That took the cake for me as my mouth hung open and the tears poured from my heart and soul. He gave me the choice, but he also gave me the ultimatum. At that moment, I gave up any fight. I was completely heartbroken. I sat and wept and could not stop. For once, he didn't comfort me but got up and left the room as I sat alone in my self-pity for hours of non-stop crying.

I ran the conversation over in my head, trying to see where I could try harder, make a better case, or change his mind. Then I came to the realization that I could not. It tore my heart apart like nothing I'd ever felt before. I could hardly catch my breath. Eventually, fatigue took over and I fell asleep. When I awoke in the late morning, Jax wasn't there. He never came back the night before. He must have slept in one of the other rooms. I got up, washed my face, which was swollen and red from all the crying, and went out to find him.

I walked into one of the rooms because the door was unlocked. There he was with one of the young, hot crew girls lying in bed. I thought the final decision was mine to make because that was how he left it, but ultimately, he made the decision for me. I knew he left that door unlocked on purpose. I knew he did what he did on purpose to teach me a hardcore lesson about not pushing him past his limits. I knew his behavior was punishment. I knew that I wouldn't recover from this. Trust was broken.

I stood at the door and just stared as Jax sat up and stared back at me. The crew girl woke up, saw me, and ran out the door like a young girl would do. He was just staring, not saying a word, and neither was I. As fresh tears easily flowed down my face, I said to him as I slowly closed the door and left the room, "You win."

It was our last day, and we hit port that evening. I threw out all of his clothes and suitcase from the bedroom, locked the door, and didn't come out. He didn't even try to come to me. I couldn't eat, so I didn't need to leave the room. I opened all the windows to invite the ocean breeze to fill the space with renewed energy. It took me the entire day to do even the simplest tasks. Several times, I broke down crying, fell asleep, woke, packed, and then repeated the exhausting cycle. Eventually, we ported.

Before departure, I took some time to soak in a hot bath, sitting in the emotional water that we had shared for the last three years. Our water. He was the river. I was the deep well. Replaying our years together, I realized how water was the same together, yet the end results could be so very different. He went one direction. I went the other. Slowly, I got dressed, pulling my hair in a ponytail because I didn't have the energy to do it. I applied no makeup and put on a ball cap and big sunglasses. I could be an adult. As I exited the room and a crew member took my luggage, I talked to the wonderful crew and thanked each of them. The young hot girl wasn't there, thankfully. Jax was already on the deck waiting for me. I exited the yacht, waved goodbye with a fake smile, and walked past Jax. I stared straight ahead and uttered not one word as I made my way to the waiting car. He followed me. I got into the car, and we left.

I rolled down the window for air and forced breath into my body. I just looked outside. I could not look at Jax. My entire body was tense with him so close to me. He sat beside me. At some point, he reached for my hand and touched it. I stared outside and coldly said, "Don't you ever touch me again."

Now, I was the mountain, immovable, staunch, and firm to the core. He removed his hand. The entire day, we traveled together without a word, a glance, a touch. Finally, I arrived at home. Jax got out with me and walked me to my door. He started to say something, but I cut him off and glared at him saying, "You changed my life for the better. I have never loved anyone like I have loved you, and I'm grateful for all of it and to you, but I never want to see you again." I walked in and closed the door as he stood staring at me with tears in his eyes. I locked the door. He walked away.

As the weeks went by, I barely got out of bed. I was in deep mourning. My closest girlfriends stepped up and checked in, calling me, letting me vent and cry for hours, dropping off food that wouldn't be eaten, and loving me unconditionally. I am forever blessed by my girlfriends.

Jax called and left messages, texted me, and kept coming back. After a month, I finally texted him that he needed to stop. I blocked him from my phone from that day forward. I didn't wait for a response. That was the end for me.

My Heart

I'd been here before. Burnt down to the ashes. Believing I wouldn't recover, wanting to end the deep, deep sorrow and unbearable pain. But I'd learned many lessons in life, and what my history had proved to me was that I would rise from those ashes time after time. I would become a stronger, better person, raising my vibration high enough to pull someone in who would be the love of my life.

I am a survivor at heart. In the end, I will always choose me. A few months later, I decided to leave. I sold my house and my furnishings and rented a storage unit for personal belongings and sentimental items. I let my family and friends know I was leaving the area for good. It was beyond time. I loved and kissed on Pepper because I was leaving her to live out her last years with my ex-husband. I dropped her off and congratulated him and his new fiancée. He is a kind, good man who deserves love and happiness. The fiancée was younger, fresher, southern, and a perfect fit for him, with a couple of kids running around. He was a family man and was excited to raise another family. Our children were adults now, one in the last years of college while the other was out in the workforce.

As I was leaving, he asked me if I was going to be okay. Thanking him, I smiled and said, "You know I'm a cat. I always land on my feet. I'll make it just fine." And as this Phoenix does, I raised myself up from the ashes of hell and flew.

When I landed, I was in Mexico. I'd rented a small place for a year outside of Punta Mita. I'd been there a few times and fantasized about living there, but now I made it a reality. I stay connected to all my family and friends back in the US. I took my time setting up the place, finding my way around, talking to locals and beginning to rebuild. In that year, I created a new space and a new life.

I met new people, made new friends, and even found a lover. He is ten years my junior. I'll never be in love with him, but he makes me feel good and gives me the companionship that I need. He is great in bed, which I think is a fast way to get over someone. Honestly, I purposely chose a younger lover, like all the men in my life had done. I wanted the experience. I wanted to know what it felt like. It turns out that someone younger isn't that big a deal.

I am growing, healing the pain, elevating my consciousness, and living life to the fullest again. I go deep within myself daily. I meditate all the time. I do the next right thing, move forward, and am learning once again how to let go. I have a tan year-round, enjoy fresh organic foods, and walk everywhere. I take fun classes, am learning Spanish, and I got my boobs lifted. I look like I'm in my forties, and I am thankful for that. My body is thin, and I work hard to keep it that way. I am starting to feel light and free again. It took a lot of pain and internal work to get me where I am.

After some time, I talked with a mutual friend of Jax and mine. Finally, I asked about Jax. Our friend asked me if I really wanted to know, and I did. He said that Jax was involved with someone after running the gamut of several women that he used and quickly discarded. No surprise there. The friend said that Jax still talked about me all the time, and did so with regret, with mourning, and with comments that he could not get over how I just cut him off and left the country.

I laughed. He still loved me. Our friend said to me gently, kindly, that he hoped I would see Jax again and talk things through. He also said he understood my position and respected it. I was glad to be so far away.

One day a few weeks after that conversation, as I was at the open market getting food, I felt a deep sensation come over me. I looked up to see Jax walking right toward me. Our mutual friend betrayed me and told him exactly where I was. My heart sank. I started to shake. I was not sure I was ready for him, or this, or us.

Jax walked right up to me without hesitation or a word, grabbed me around my waist, pulled me into him, and kissed me. I naturally submitted to him, as I always had. My body ignited with fire, my heart beat fast, and my mind analyzed the situation. My mind was supposed to protect me. I felt all the flame and passion that had always been there, but something was missing now.

I realized in that moment that I am a flowing river, too, one that moves forward not backward. I'd grown again, rising to a higher consciousness. My needs and wants had changed; my path was clear. No matter what Jax said or did, I knew in that second that I wouldn't go back to him.

I let go of the lover after I saw Jax. With great passion and familiarity, I slept with Jax like he was my old sweetheart from college. Again, there was so much love and satisfaction. We talked through all things, but this time I didn't waiver.

The roles were reversed. I had moved on in my life. This scenario was like looking in the mirror again, but he was me, and I was him. Two sides of the same coin, together but apart. Twin flames forever bound.

The love will always be there, but the time had come to an end. The lessons were learned, growth had maxed out, and the energy levels had shifted, for both of us. I will be drawn to him forever. There's an invisible magnet between us—a love that goes to the bottom of the water well. But water moves forward, and so will I.

I didn't go back to him. I loved him all over again when I was with him during that short visit, finally meeting him where he wanted me to all along. I understood what he meant by being "in the present." So, in the present, I gave him my all, but the moment he left, I let go completely. He understood it was over.

We both cried at the truth and the reality of our lives, once together and now apart. The closure came for both of us, so we could move on in our lives once and for all.

My Future

I spent the rest of my time in Mexico planning how to move forward in my life and preparing to go back home. I began my search for where to live in the US. I was not going back to Atlanta. For years, I'd wanted to find the healthy balance of a smaller city with all its modern appeal but an easier, simpler, calmer way of life. I'd taken time to look all over the southern US, in Tennessee, North Carolina, South Carolina, Alabama, and Northern Florida. Ultimately, I fell in love with the South Carolina coast. I reread notes from my visits and remembered the feeling of how the small country towns outside of Charleston pulled at my heartstrings.

I reached out to a Charleston-area realtor known for relocation. I explained that I had wrapped up my time in Mexico and would arrive in six weeks. I'd stay with a friend in Atlanta, basically to drop off my luggage, and then head to Charleston for a week's stay. It was time to settle and to start fresh. This time, I would go with the clear realization that I may be spending the rest of my life alone, and I'd have to get comfortable with that.

I decided to give up on dating. I decided not to look for any relationship with a man unless it was friendship. What is the point? I have let go of the romantic fantasy I created in my head. I have accepted the facts. I'd had my one love and was sure the universe wouldn't provide another. How could it, for I had all that I wanted with one? And I am thankful.

I am at peace knowing that I will not have my heart broken again. I am strong, independent, and resilient. I love my solitude, so I will just accept the occasional loneliness. I will be just fine. I know I will never break my heart. I am excited. Happiness overflows from me, my energy is high with renewed hope. I am back. Grounded.

Made in the USA
Columbia, SC
06 July 2022

62906267R00085